# COLE STEELE
# ASYLUM

# ONE

It was the unusual blend of sheer paranoia and the uncanny ability to remain inconspicuous that caught Shaun Tolliver's attention. He first spotted him while rifling through a rack of jeans at the Greenwood Mall; a man standing out, not due to his appearance, but because of the overt interest two poorly dressed men displayed in him.

Peter Stroebel. A name the world knew little of. Living in Nashville under an alias, he was thousands of miles away from his homeland. He had been a beacon of hope once, the campaign manager for an upstart political movement in Russia that threatened to unseat the entrenched power structure. But when two of his closest associates met untimely deaths, Stroebel understood the consequences of standing against the Kremlin.

His journey from Russia was a tale in itself - a daring drive from Moscow to the border, a cloak-and-dagger exchange with smugglers, and a harrowing journey culminating in a Miami port. Eventually, he sought refuge within Nashville's small Slavic community, where he invested his remaining money into a scooter and bike rental shop - "Spree."

In the mall, Peter's need for a fresh start led him to explore the clothing racks while Shaun hunted for the perfect outfit for his date with his gym crush. As a former convict turned investigator, Shaun's keen eye couldn't help but notice the two men closely observing Peter. Something about them screamed danger - not of the law enforcement type, but something more insidious.

On a hunch, Shaun followed them into the parking lot, his heart pounding in his chest as the two men pulled out silenced pistols. Without thinking, Shaun roared his black Audi into action, narrowly missing the two assailants. Swinging the car beside Peter, Shaun called out, "Bro, get in. Those guys don't look like the type that give up easily."

Bewildered, Peter hesitated before scrambling into the car, just as the men in pursuit regained their bearings. The car chase was something straight out of an action movie, their pursuers hot on their heels through the winding streets of Nashville. Shaun's deft driving shook off their tail, but the respite was brief.

Suddenly, their world jolted as a car struck them from the side, sending the Audi into a spin and crashing into a guardrail on a bridge. The pursuers emerged, ditching their firearms into the river below. Shaun cursed under his breath. It was over. Or so he thought until the flashing lights of a police cruiser washed over them.

With their pursuers apprehended and a tow truck on the way, Shaun took a moment to breathe. The adrenaline of the chase was beginning to ebb, replaced with a cold dread. Glancing at his silent companion, Shaun had to ask, "On a scale of one to ten, how much trouble are you in?"

Peter simply responded, "I don't know what you mean."

He would soon find out. Little did he know, this chance encounter at the mall was just the beginning of a dangerous game of cat and mouse. Their lives had intertwined, and the race to evade the Kremlin's reach had begun.

# TWO

Shaun's phone vibrated, the caller ID flashing Lori's name. He accepted the call, holding the sleek device to his ear. The ambient sounds of sirens and a distant city hum played softly in the background.

"Never guess where I am," Shaun began, trying to lighten the mood.

"Jail's out because you're on your cellphone," Lori's voice was equal parts exasperation and amusement.

Shaun chuckled, "Can't get anything past you."

There was a brief pause on the other end, and then, with a sigh of foreknowledge, Lori inquired, "Does it involve the police, Shaun?"

"Ladies and gentlemen, we have a winner!" He replied, making it sound like a game show announcement.

"Ugh, what happened?" Lori's concern was evident.

"Fender bender. We're on the bridge."

The "we" seemed to catch Lori's attention. "Who's 'we'?"

Shaun hesitated for a moment, glancing at Peter, "That's... complicated. But a story for another time."

"You're not making this easy, Shaun," Lori remarked, her voice now softer, tinged with concern.

"Never said I would," Shaun grinned, even though he knew she couldn't see it. "Hey, any chance you can come pick us up?"

There was a brief silence. "Alright, I'm on my way. But you owe me big time, little brother."

"Just add it to my tab."

Lori chuckled, "It's getting pretty lengthy. Be there soon. Text me your exact location."

"Will do. Thanks, Sis."

The call ended, and Shaun looked at Peter, "Relax. We've got a ride coming. Though there will be a lot of questions you'll need to answer."

Peter nodded slowly, his gaze fixed on the horizon, deep in thought. "Thank you."

Shaun smiled, "Just another day in the life." But he knew, as the weight of the day's events began to settle, that things were far from ordinary. And they were only just beginning.

## THREE

The rain's percussion against the car roof added a melancholic backdrop, as the trio navigated the wet streets. The glow from the city lights reflected off the glistening roads, casting shadows that played like old film footage on the car windows.

"Didn't you just get this car?" Lori asked, her voice infused with a mix of curiosity and sympathy.

Shaun sighed, running a hand through his slightly damp hair, "Yeah, and just finished paying it off too."

Lori turned a gaze towards the rearview mirror, trying to decipher the enigma that was Peter. His presence, both silent and imposing, filled the car with questions neither sibling was ready to confront. It was clear Peter had experienced something heavy, something that weighed on him.

The rhythmic sweep of the windshield wipers worked overtime to clear the incessant rain, creating a hypnotic motion. Yet, amidst the downpour, Lori's acute sense of observation caught Peter's rather antiquated style of clothing. It looked like something he'd owned for years. And the shopping bag he'd left behind in the parking lot explained the obvious lack of any contemporary attire.

"Where'd you come from?" Lori's question was open-ended, though she had a good idea about her brother's whereabouts.

Shaun smirked, "The mall. I had a date to dress up for."

Lori's eyebrow raised playfully, "I was referring to our silent friend back there."

"I figured. But like I said, he's not one for words," Shaun shot back, a smirk playing on his lips.

With a softer, more compassionate tone, Lori addressed Peter, "Hey, it's okay. You can talk to us. Where would you like to go?"

Peter remained unresponsive for a moment, his gaze fixed on the rain-smeared window. When he finally spoke, his voice was laced with a tiredness that transcended mere physical exhaustion. "Downtown, please."

"Downtown's a broad place," Lori replied gently, her eyes flicking to the rearview mirror. "Any specific spot?"

Peter hesitated. Then, almost in a whisper, "Near the Slavic district."

Lori nodded, understanding dawning on her. Every city had its sanctuaries, places where people from different parts of the world congregated for the comfort of shared memories and familiar tongues. The Slavic district in Nashville was one such place. It was clear that Peter was looking for a haven, a place to hide, to heal. And as the rain continued its relentless pour, the car moved steadily towards a destination that promised safety, but perhaps, also, a deeper entanglement in a web of international intrigue.

# FOUR

Lori parked the car a few blocks away from an unassuming apartment complex, its gray façade reminiscent of Soviet-era architecture. The soft glow of neon lights from a nearby pawn shop provided the only illumination, casting an eerie hue on the rain-slicked streets.

"Thanks for the lift," Peter said, his voice edged with caution.

Shaun squinted into the rearview mirror. "You sure you'll be okay?"

Peter gave a tight-lipped nod. "I've been in worse spots. Just stay safe. And thank you." With that, he exited the vehicle, taking long strides toward his destination, a figure of intrigue disappearing into the night.

As the car pulled away, Lori couldn't contain her curiosity. "He's hiding something."

Shaun smirked. "Isn't everyone?"

Lori rolled her eyes but then a thought struck her. "The cameras."

A nod from Shaun. He'd been thinking the same thing. Pulling out a compact device, a modern-day miracle of surveillance tech, Shaun focused it on Peter's building. It wasn't precisely eavesdropping; it was more about ensuring a man they'd saved wasn't walking into another trap.

The apartment was austere, a stark contrast to the vibrant streets of Nashville. Walls were decorated with vintage posters from Russian rock bands of the '80s. Peter moved to a desk by the window, and a bank of monitors blinked to life.

Lori watched closely as Peter started making coffee, seemingly to ground himself. But the real revelation was his swift review of footage from discreet cameras he'd installed around the building. High-end tech, a nod to the life he'd been hiding.

The two Russian operatives from earlier came into view. Their presence hours before the mall incident now undeniable.

"Damn," Shaun murmured, "He's in deeper than we thought."

Peter's on-screen expression darkened. He quickly packed a few essentials, likely readying to move to a secondary location.

"We should keep an eye on him," Lori whispered.

Shaun agreed. "But from a distance. If those guys come after him again, we need to be ready."

The rain lessened to a drizzle, the car's engine idling softly. In the distance, the muted sounds of the city continued, a reminder that beneath its surface, secrets always lurked.

## FIVE

The ambient hum of Peter's laptop and the distant murmur of early morning traffic created a comfortable cocoon of normalcy as he typed, a buffer against the world outside. His blog, a mosaic of political revelations and hard truths, was his silent rebellion. Each keystroke was a calculated move on the chessboard of political warfare.

He paused, rereading the last paragraph and pondering a more biting adjective when an interruption flashed onto his screen. A news alert. For a moment, his heart raced, fearing the news was about him. The headline left him frozen:

*"Prominent Chechen Dissident Assassinated in Switzerland"*

The article painted a chilling picture. An outspoken Chechen, known for his vocal criticism of the Kremlin's dominion over the region, had met an eerie end. The man had been poisoned with a nerve agent, stealthily delivered through the air vents of his rental car. Within hours, his respiratory system failed, leaving him motionless on a quiet Swiss road.

Peter's thoughts raced back to a previous case. He remembered how the world had watched, horrified, as two victims struggled for their lives. The parallels were unmistakable. The audacity of the Kremlin, using such a method on foreign soil, was a grim testament to their ruthless reach.

Digging further into the article, Peter found a thread of hope. The assassins had made a mistake. CCTV footage from a posh ski resort had captured them, and their faces were splashed across European news. Cross-referencing these images led investigators to a hotel in Italy where they had checked in using false names, but the trail was crystal clear.

Though the international community reacted with outrage, Peter knew all too well the real message: the Kremlin's reach was vast, their memory long, and their retaliation swift.

He bookmarked the article and closed the tab, the weight of realization pressing on his shoulders. His fingers hesitated over the keyboard, questioning if his writings were a beacon of hope or a spotlight drawing danger ever closer. Taking a deep breath, he resumed his work. Now, more than ever, his voice was vital.

The muted tones of dawn began filtering through his blinds, casting the room in a soft, golden hue. But for Peter, the world outside had never felt colder.

## SIX

The Sun Diner, tucked in a busy corner of downtown Nashville, was abuzz with the morning crowd. Its iconic art-deco style façade, complete with neon signage, beckoned to both locals and tourists alike. Inside, golden records adorned the walls, a nod to the city's rich musical heritage. The rich aroma of coffee hung in the air, blending seamlessly with the clatter of dishes and muffled conversations. It was an atmosphere that promised warmth, good food, and a touch of nostalgia.

Shaun and Lori sat in a booth towards the back, a vantage point that gave them a clear view of the entrance. Between them, a spread of scrambled eggs, crispy bacon, and buttery toast lay untouched, the aftermath of the previous evening casting a shadow over their appetite.

Taking a sip from his coffee mug, Shaun glanced around. He recognized a few faces—Judge Martinez engrossed in the morning paper, Attorney Reese animatedly discussing something with her client.

Lori, her brow furrowed, was the first to break the silence. "You sure know how to pick your shopping trips. What on earth happened last night?"

Shaun took a deep breath. "Just wanted a new shirt for the date. Then things got... complicated. That man—Peter, he was being targeted."

Lori's eyes scanned Shaun's face, searching for signs of exaggeration. "Targeted? As in, an assassination attempt?"

Shaun nodded, "Russian operatives, from the looks of it."

She shook her head in disbelief, "This is Nashville, not some international spy thriller."

Shaun shrugged, taking a bite of toast, "Reality's stranger than fiction, sis."

They sat in contemplation, the gravity of the situation settling in. Lori finally said, "That's not a random act, Shaun. If they were FSB, this is huge."

He leaned back, "Seems our Mr. Peter wasn't just another face in the crowd. He's involved in something big."

Lori took a moment, then said, "You did good, saving him. But this could get dangerous."

Shaun gave a half-smile, "Isn't that part of the job description for us Tollivers?"

Lori gave a soft chuckle, "Still, stay sharp. And keep me in the loop."

"Speaking of loops," Shaun interjected, looking a bit sheepish, "Can you take me to the lot later? I forgot something in my car."

Lori raised an eyebrow, "Seriously?"

Shaun grinned, "Might've been a bit distracted, you think?"

With a roll of her eyes and a smile, Lori relented, "Alright, let's finish breakfast first."

Amid the chaos of the previous night, the simple pleasure of breakfast with family was a beacon of normalcy. But both knew, things in Nashville had just taken a decidedly dangerous turn.

## SEVEN

The Nashville sun shimmered upon rows of gleaming vehicles as Shaun and Lori drove into the dealership lot. Situated adjacent was the body shop—a hive of activity as mechanics bustled around, examining dents, replacing parts, and spraying new coats of paint. A radio somewhere played country tunes, and the distant hum of a pneumatic wrench filled the air.

"I hate leaving my car at places like this," Shaun murmured, his gaze drifting towards where his black Audi sat, sandwiched between a crumpled hatchback and a luxury SUV.

"Well, it's better here than in the river," Lori quipped, pulling into a parking spot.

Shaun approached his car, spotting the familiar shopping bag in the passenger seat. As he reached to retrieve it, his eyes caught a glimpse of something else—an unfamiliar cellphone lying on the backseat.

"What've you got there?" Lori called out, peering over the car's roof.

"Looks like a burner," Shaun replied, holding up the device for her to see.

"Your friend?" Lori asked, her tone dripping with a mix of intrigue and sarcasm.

"The great conversationalist," Shaun shot back with a smirk.

"Think he'll want it back?"

Before Shaun could answer, the phone rang. The unexpected sound caused Shaun's fingers to tighten around its thin frame. Lori's eyes widened. "You going to answer it?"

"Should I?" Shaun hesitated, staring at the unknown number flashing on the screen.

"Maybe it's him. Calling from another phone," Lori speculated.

Taking a deep breath, Shaun pressed the green icon. "Hello?"

A female voice, sharp and urgent, rattled off in Russian. The cadence was fast and filled with what sounded like anxiety or maybe anger.

Lori watched Shaun's puzzled face, silently mouthing, "Who is it?"

Shaun could only shrug in response. A beat later, the line fell silent. The woman had hung up.

"I don't know," Shaun admitted, his brow furrowing. "It was in Russian, I think. She didn't sound happy."

Lori smirked. "Maybe it was his girlfriend."

Shaun chuckled, "Soon to be ex, judging by that tone. Honestly, I wouldn't have gotten a word in even if I spoke her language."

Lori sighed, looking over Shaun's damaged Audi. "Now what?"

"We need to go car shopping."

She shot him a stern look. "No, *you* need to go by yourself. I have a hearing to prepare for."

"That the dog bite guy?" Shaun teased, his eyes twinkling with mischief.

Lori nodded, trying to keep her expression neutral. "Yes."

"I don't need to be there again, do I?" Shaun continued, his grin growing wider.

Lori rolled her eyes. "I think we're good."

"Guy gets bit by a chihuahua and acts like he was mauled by a lion," Shaun laughed.

Lori smirked, "It did bite him in the scrotum."

Shaun cringed, "I really don't want to know why or how that happened."

With a sly smile, Lori reminded, "The dog's owner is his ex-wife."

Shaun shook his head, laughing, "That might explain it."

Their laughter echoed across the lot, a brief moment of levity in the midst of the storm they'd unwittingly entered.

## EIGHT

Peter woke with a start, sweat beading his forehead, his heart pounding like a drum in his chest. The cheap mattress of his clandestine apartment seemed to cling to him, holding him in a nightmare he could neither fully remember nor completely forget.

The room was a Spartan space, adorned only with the essentials: a desk stacked with an array of tech gadgets, a wardrobe full of inconspicuous clothing, and a set of weights in the corner for what passed as exercise in his cramped quarters.

Flashbacks of his tumultuous flight to America gnawed at his waking moments. The silent agony of leaving family behind, instructing them to hide—no goodbyes, no promises—was a laceration to his soul that never fully healed.

For a split second, he imagined his mother's voice, soft and comforting. It was always a phone call away, a tether to another world. A burner phone—simple, disposable, untraceable.

His eyes widened. *The burner phone.*

He sat up as if electrocuted, scanning his modest apartment. Desk—no. Nightstand—no. Drawers hastily pulled open, their contents dumped, revealed no sign of the phone.

His mind sprinted back to the shopping trip. Had he taken the phone with him? Was it in the bag he'd left in the parking lot? Or even worse, in the car with that guy, Shaun? An inferno of panic roared through him.

He looked at his laptop—more bad news. A notification blinked, telling him one of his bike rentals had exited its usual district. *Something else to deal with,* he thought, but it paled in importance to the missing phone.

*They could trace it,* he thought. *They could find my family.*

A torrent of images assaulted him: shadowy figures forcing their way into his parents' hideout, his sister screaming, the cold, ruthless eyes of the men he knew would be sent to retrieve them. He shook his head violently, trying to dispel the visions.

*Focus.*

Peter knew what he had to do. Retrace his steps. From the mall, to the accident, to the impromptu lift from Shaun and Lori. He needed to find that phone before it became the loose thread that unraveled his precariously stitched-together life.

So he rose, his body stiff from a night of troubled sleep but adrenalized by a sense of dire urgency. Every second counted now. He grabbed a jacket, avoiding the mirror as he exited the apartment. No time for reflections; there were already too many haunting him.

In the world of hunted men, he knew there was no such thing as caution; there was only lesser degrees of risk. And right now, the greatest risk of all was doing nothing.

His mind made up, Peter stepped out, locking his door behind him. The stakes were incalculably high, but what choice did he have?

The burner phone was no longer just a means of communication. It had become the lifeline he was desperate to hold onto, the only thing that connected him to everything he had sacrificed. And he would be damned if he let it slip through his fingers.

## NINE

Peter sank into a booth at Dough Bird, a casual eatery where pizza met rotisserie. The exposed brick walls, rustic wooden tables, and industrial-style lighting gave the place a hip but welcoming feel. He looked at the menu, perusing items like "Spicy Korean Wings" and "Prime Rib French Dip," but he had no appetite. An Uber had dropped him off, and now he was just killing time, strategizing his next move.

Outside, his car sat forlorn in a parking lot, slapped with an orange "abandoned vehicle" sticker. Part of him wanted to sweep the car for anything incriminating, but he knew that was a futile gesture. If they wanted to find him, they already had ways. His priority was the missing burner phone, his fragile lifeline to the world he'd left behind.

Glancing at his wristwatch, Peter calculated the minutes. He needed to reach the mall the moment it swung open its doors for the day. Paying for his untouched coffee, he thanked the waiter and hailed another Uber.

When he arrived at the mall, the atmosphere felt almost eerie. Many of the storefronts were still engulfed in darkness, and the halls were quiet except for the occasional clatter of a janitorial cart. His footsteps echoed ominously as he walked, filling the vast, empty space with the sound of his own anxiety.

Finally, he reached the dimly lit store where he'd last been. Even in the low light, the outline of a mannequin in the window looked like a sentinel, standing guard over lost opportunities and vanished time.

The door clicked open. A young woman, perhaps in her late twenties, flashed a cheerful smile. "Good morning!"

"Do you have a lost and found?" Peter's voice was tinged with urgency.

"Ah, not much of one," she chuckled. "But you're welcome to look. Wait at the counter; I'll get our box of forgotten items."

As he waited, light music trickled from the store's sound system, filling the room like an auditory wallpaper. Moments later, she returned with a box, its contents a jumble of mismatched gloves, random keys, and a handful of cheap umbrellas.

Peter searched through it quickly, his hands trembling slightly. No phone. His heart sank.

"I'm sorry we couldn't help," the woman said, sensing his disappointment.

"Thank you," Peter replied. His thoughts drifted back to that dodgy Miami store where he'd bought the burner, a place that smelled of stale alcohol and desperation. He'd felt a sliver of safety then, a tiny anchor in a turbulent sea. Now, it was gone.

His heart was racing as he left the store. *How did they find me?* The audacity of an attack on U.S. soil was unsettling. And yet, nothing in the news. No whispers, no ripples, no clues. It was as if it hadn't happened at all.

Peter felt like a man standing on a crumbling cliff. Below him, an abyss. Above him, a storm. And in his hand, an empty line that had once been a lifeline, now leading nowhere. It was a terrifying moment of isolation, a realization that he was profoundly, devastatingly alone.

## TEN

Lori was engrossed in her laptop screen, rifling through digital pages of case notes. Her fingers were a blur on the keyboard when Shaun walked in, immediately catching her attention.

He'd just parked his new black Audi R8 in the lot, a machine that was as much a work of art as it was a vehicle. With its distinctive grille, R8 badging, and full LED headlights with Audi laser light, it looked like it belonged on the set of a Hollywood action film rather than in the lot of a law firm. The sculpted side blades and sloping contours whispered promises of power, embodying the peak of Audi engineering and design. It was luxury and performance encapsulated in high-gloss Carbon Sigma. The car was not just a car; it was an audacious statement.

"I see that your car shopping was a success," Lori noted, lifting an eyebrow.

"You like?" Shaun grinned, a touch of smug satisfaction in his voice.

"Personally, I would have been a little more modest and lighter on the wallet," Lori said, feigning a look of disapproval.

"I got a good deal on it," Shaun defended himself.

Then her eyes shifted to the object in his hand—the burner phone. "That our friend's?"

Shaun looked down at the phone and nodded. "Yes."

"Has anyone else called?" Lori prodded, her eyes narrowing.

"No, just the Russian female from the other day. But there have been texts that were obviously not in English," Shaun reported.

"You know, with everything that happened, I haven't seen or heard anything in the news or on the internet," Lori said, her tone tinged with incredulity.

"Yeah, it's strange. It was all a blur—one minute I'm shopping, and the next..." Shaun's voice trailed off as his thoughts seemed to catch in his throat.

Just then, a knock on the door interrupted their exchange. The door swung open, and there he was—Shaun's ex-parole officer, standing awkwardly in the threshold, his expression a mix of concern and professional detachment. A cold silence filled the room, and Lori could almost hear Shaun's pulse quicken.

This was not a random visit. This was not coincidental. And suddenly, the world around them seemed to fold into razor-sharp focus. Lori and Shaun exchanged a look that said what words could not:

*The past is never really past, and sometimes it knocks on your door.*

# ELEVEN

Mitchell Payne stood in the doorway, imposing and uninvited. The creases on his forehead suggested years of scrutinizing parolees like Shaun. He had the kind of face that was already set in a frown, even when he was attempting to smile. His crew-cut hairstyle screamed military, or maybe 'I-mean-business' in the world of parole officers.

Shaun broke the silence first. "You must miss the feeling of a warm cup of piss in your hand. I have to warn you that I'm out of practice—accuracy might be an issue." Shaun hated the drug testing and it's lack of privacy.

A vein pulsed in Payne's forehead as his jaw tightened, but he fought off the instinctual reaction. "Just a follow-up," he said, softening his tone. "I heard about a fender-bender on the bridge. Your name came up."

Shaun glanced through the window at his shiny new Audi, then back at Payne. "I'm fine, had to replace my car though. Appreciate the concern."

"The guys down at the station say some witnesses to the accident could've sworn the other car was pursuing you," Payne continued, his eyes narrowing.

"Maybe it was the paparazzi," Shaun fired back. "I do work for one of Nashville's most popular attorneys, after all."

That was the moment Lori decided to step in. "Cut to the chase, Payne. We're a little busy this morning."

Payne looked back and forth between Shaun and Lori, his eyes like laser beams. "Just concerned that my former parolee here might be slipping."

"Tell you what, Payne," Shaun smirked, "if I get the urge to break the law, you'll be the first one I'll call."

It was Lori's turn to stare down Payne. "Every minute you stand in my office is one less that I have to offer my clients who expect nothing less than quality representation. In fact, a reasonable person might call this harassment, loitering..."

"Stay out of trouble, Shaun," Payne finally grumbled, his voice tinged with begrudging respect.

As Payne took a few steps toward the door, Shaun couldn't resist a parting shot. "You sure you don't want a cup for the road?"

The door slammed shut behind Payne, and the atmosphere in the room relaxed just a fraction. Lori turned to Shaun, her eyes still flickering with residual irritation.

"You don't know when to quit, do you?"

Shaun grinned, unrepentant. "Where's the fun in that?"

Lori shook her head. "Sometimes I wonder if you're addicted to risk."

He leaned in closer, meeting her eyes. "Only when the reward is worth it."

Shaun Tolliver looked down again at the cellular device in his hand. It was ringing again.

# TWELVE

The diner was a slice of Americana—red vinyl booths, checkered floor tiles, a jukebox in the corner belting out country classics. The smell of bacon and freshly brewed coffee filled the air. At a booth near the back, two men sat facing each other. They wore jeans and cowboy boots, their casual wear calculated to blend seamlessly into the southern tableau.

"More coffee?" the waitress asked, her accent laying on the Southern charm.

"Sure, darling," the taller of the two men replied, his own accent a well-practiced drawl. She filled their mugs, and as she walked away, the man's eyes followed her for a moment before snapping back to his partner.

"We need to finish this," the shorter one said. His name was Anton, and while his English was impeccable, his eyes had the icy calculation of a man who didn't grow up on football and apple pie.

"I know, I know," replied his partner, Viktor. "But we can't afford to be sloppy. Not with Stroebel. He's slippery, and he knows he's a target."

Anton took a sip of his coffee, his eyes meeting Viktor's. "We can't go back empty-handed. You know what the Kremlin will do to us. Worse, what they'll do to our families."

"Then let's make sure we don't go back empty-handed," Viktor said, pulling out a phone and placing it on the table. The screen lit up with an encrypted message. "Our contact says Stroebel will be in the downtown area tomorrow."

Anton raised an eyebrow. "You trust this information? That area is always crowded. Too many witnesses."

Viktor smirked. "Which is why it's the perfect place. He'll feel safe, relaxed. We get in, blend with the crowd, do the job, and get out. A couple of guys in a tragic accident. Could happen to anyone."

"We've been in America too long," Anton mused. "You're starting to think like them."

Viktor grinned, but his eyes were cold. "Thinking like them is how we'll beat them. And how we'll finally get Stroebel."

Both men nodded, a silent pact forming between them. The weight of their mission was far more substantial than any breakfast they could order. And neither could afford the luxury of failure.

As they left the diner, Viktor looked back one last time, as if memorizing the details—the red vinyl booths, the checkered tiles, the jukebox.

If all went according to plan, they'd never see this place—or any other part of America—again.

And for that, they felt neither regret nor relief—only a chilling focus on the grim task at hand.

## THIRTEEN

Shaun Tolliver felt a prickling sensation on the back of his neck as the phone line went dead. He looked at Lori, her eyes wide with the realization that they had stumbled into something far more serious than they'd anticipated.

"That sounded like Peter's mother," Lori said, her voice tinged with apprehension.

"Could be. Either way, she's panicking. If what she says is true, then Peter isn't just running from something, he's got family worrying about him too."

Shaun put the phone down on Lori's glass-top desk, filled with legal books and a desktop computer that blinked silently in the hushed atmosphere of the room. Lori's eyes moved from the phone to Shaun, then to the window that offered a glimpse of his new acquisition—his sleek black Audi R8.

It was a car that screamed success, luxury, and a thirst for speed. With its prominent wheel arches and distinctive side blades, it had an aerodynamic silhouette that cut through the air as smoothly as it cut through traffic. The R8 was a performance masterpiece, boasting a V10 engine and a top speed that most wouldn't dare to reach. Shaun had found his new adrenaline fix, and it was parked just outside the office.

But right now, the Audi, as fascinating as it was, wasn't the focal point. The burner phone was.

"You think we should call her back?" Lori asked, breaking the silence.

"Doing so might get her into trouble. Heck, it might get us into more trouble," Shaun replied, recalling the previous confrontation with his ex-parole officer, Mitchell Payne. Payne would love to catch him on the wrong side of any situation.

Shaun continued, "I think we should try to find Peter first. If we can get the phone back to him, he'll be the one best suited to handle his own affairs."

Lori rubbed her temples. "Yeah, but how are we going to find him? All we know is that he narrowly escaped two men who were probably trying to kill him."

Shaun picked up the phone and swiped through it. "He received some texts, also in Russian. Maybe we can get them translated."

Lori raised her eyebrows, a glimmer of hope in her eyes. "That could work, and it might give us a lead on where to find him."

At that moment, the phone buzzed, and a new text message appeared. Shaun read the Cyrillic characters aloud, not comprehending their meaning but understanding the urgency. He looked up at Lori.

"Things are moving fast. We need to move faster."

Lori nodded. "Agreed. But first things first, let's get these texts translated. Then we go find Peter, and God willing, we help him before whoever is chasing him catches up."

The room was filled with a sense of urgency now, like a fuse had been lit, and time was running out. They both felt it, the gravity of something bigger than themselves, pulling them into a situation that was spiraling rapidly out of control.

"We're not spies," Lori said, as if trying to convince herself.

Shaun grinned. "Maybe it's time for a career change."

Their eyes met, and in that instant, they silently agreed to embark on a journey that was as dangerous as it was uncertain. And yet, there was no turning back. The dice had been rolled, and the game was afoot.

Both knew they were stepping over a line, a boundary that separated their everyday lives from the world of international intrigue and deadly secrets. But some lines, once crossed, redefine who you are.

# FOURTEEN

Viktor and Anton stood like statues, their eyes hidden behind dark sunglasses, scanning the pedestrians passing by. They had cowboy boots, faded jeans, and plaid shirts that made them look as American as anyone else wandering around downtown Nashville.

Behind them loomed the Nissan Stadium, home to thrills, spills, and the kind of American spectacle that could make you forget about the world's troubles. If you squinted across the Cumberland River, you could make out the spires of the AT&T Building, popularly known as the "Batman Building" thanks to its distinctive, gothic architecture.

Viktor's satellite phone buzzed, vibrating in his hand. A sense of anticipation filled the air, electric and palpable, as he answered the call. As soon as he heard the Russian voice on the other end, his posture stiffened, his fingers clenched around the phone a little tighter.

Hearing his native tongue was like tasting a slice of home, sweet and familiar. "Dah, we will have completed this soon. We will not fail," Viktor assured the voice, crisply formal even in the informal setting.

The voice on the other end crackled with an aura of authority, as if the man could command legions through the phone alone. "You better not. The Kremlin is watching. Your orders were clear. Eliminate Peter Stroebel. Do you have any leads?"

Anton glanced at Viktor, his eyes barely visible through the tinted shades, his face as unreadable as a blank page. He too was feeling the heat, the kind that could turn a mission into a deadly trap.

Viktor responded, "We are close. Very close. It's only a matter of time before we find him."

"See that you do. We cannot afford any more delays. Failure is not an option. And do remember, if you're caught or killed, the government will disavow any knowledge of your actions. Do I make myself clear?"

Crystal clear, Viktor thought but didn't dare to say out loud. "Understood," was all he allowed himself to utter before hanging up.

As he ended the call, Viktor felt the weight of the mission pressing down on him like a hundred-pound anvil. This was bigger than him, bigger than Anton, and even bigger than the two agents who were given a simple, albeit ruthless, mission.

"We cannot fail," Anton finally broke his silence, his voice carrying a tremor of uncertainty for the first time. "Too much is at stake."

Viktor looked at Anton, then back at the shimmering waters of the Cumberland River, thinking about the life he'd left behind, a life he would never get back if he failed this mission.

"Failure isn't in our vocabulary," Viktor replied, the contours of his lips pulling into a grim smile. "Besides, we have the element of surprise."

"We won't, if we wait any longer. Time is running out," Anton said, checking his wristwatch as if it could fast-forward them to the success they desperately needed.

"You're right. Let's go find our target. We have a job to complete."

The two men melded back into the American tapestry, two souls hidden behind a façade of cowboy boots and denim jeans. They walked away, the soles of their boots hitting the pavement in rhythmic unison, each step taking them closer to their objective—and a collision course with destiny.

As they moved, Viktor couldn't shake off a nagging feeling, an itch he couldn't scratch. He knew that their window was closing, that every ticking second took away a sliver of the advantage they had.

They had to act fast.

After all, even in the city of music, not all notes are played to the tune of love and joy. Some carried the heavy timbre of dread, and it was a tune Viktor and Anton were becoming increasingly familiar with.

Failure, as they had been reminded, was not an option. And so they vanished into the thrum of the city, two shadows swallowed whole, leaving behind nothing but the chilling trace of a threat yet realized.

# FIFTEEN

Peter Stroebel stared at his laptop, his fingers tapping a restless rhythm on the edge of the keyboard. On the screen, GPS markers indicated the locations of his growing fleet of rideshare bikes and electric scooters strewn across downtown Nashville. All except one. One little dot was far removed from the herd, an anomaly in a system Peter had spent months perfecting.

Peter had gotten into this rideshare business under a veil of near-anonymity. A couple of Skype calls, some swift crypto transactions, and boom—he was the owner of a micro-mobility fleet. The service was like Bird, but smaller, more grassroots. It allowed him to send money back to his family, all the while keeping him hidden in the veil of digital transactions.

And yet, anonymity had its pitfalls.

He clicked on the rogue dot, bringing up its last known coordinates. Looked like someone might be playing the finder's fee game—hoarding his bike until a desperate search triggered a reward offer. People did all sorts of things for a quick buck, and Peter couldn't blame them.

He had more pressing concerns.

Like the missing burner phone, an untraceable line that was as important to his safety as the air he breathed. It had slipped from his grasp during the high-speed chase, a lapse that still gnawed at him.

He closed his laptop, slid it into a leather messenger bag, and zipped it shut. Time to find that stray bike and perhaps claim a piece of normalcy back from the chaos of the last few days.

Scooping up a business-only smartphone from the table, he mounted one of his own electric bikes parked outside the building. With a flick of the wrist, he was off, racing down the streets of Nashville like a shadow fleeing the dawn.

As he rode, the wind cut across his face, a feeling of liberation that stood in stark contrast to the burden on his mind. The missing phone, the Russian agents, and the mounting questions—all of it tugged at his focus, like background noise rising in volume.

When he arrived at the rogue bike's coordinates, Peter's eyes scanned the area. There it was, tucked away behind a dilapidated warehouse, its frame glinting in the sun as if taunting him for taking so long to find it.

He parked his bike, approaching the stray. As he got closer, his eyes narrowed. Something was off. The bike wasn't just parked; it was carefully positioned, almost deliberately hidden from the casual observer.

His instincts screamed at him, goosebumps pricking his skin. He reached into his pocket, clutching the business phone. A simple device, incapable of international calls, unconnected to his past life.

Yet, right at that moment, it rang. Unknown number.

He hesitated for a split second, debating whether to answer. And in that fraction of a second, Peter Stroebel made a choice. A choice that would change the trajectory of his life forever.

He tapped the screen, lifting the phone to his ear. "Hello?"

No reply.

"Hello?" he said again, the tension mounting, each second stretching into an eternity.

Then, from the other end, a voice spoke. A voice that sent a shiver down his spine.

"We know where you are."

The line went dead.

Peter looked around, his eyes darting in every direction. An empty street, a distant skyline, and a hidden bike—that's all he saw. But he knew better.

He was not alone.

And in that chilling realization, Peter Stroebel understood one thing with frightening clarity: The wheels of fate had just taken a perilous turn, thrusting him into a high-stakes game he never signed up for.

He mounted his bike and pedaled as fast as he could. He had to disappear, blend into the city's pulsating heart, become just another dot on someone else's screen. Because in the grand scheme of things, that's what he had always been—a mere dot, a fragment of a much larger and deadlier puzzle.

As his bike ate up the distance, Peter couldn't shake off the feeling that his past was catching up to him, rolling in like a storm cloud, darker and more menacing with each passing second. And there was no outrunning this storm.

Not this time.

## SIXTEEN

Viktor and Anton trailed Peter like wolves stalking a wounded deer. They were parked a block away when he abandoned his wayward bike. Their eyes, cold and calculating, remained fixated on the prey. They had let him slip through their fingers once, and there would not be a second time.

Their dark sedan purred in muted ferocity, waiting to pounce, as they tailed Peter through the latticework of streets. Traffic was a flowing river of steel and rubber, but like water receding from a shore, it began to thin as they neared an intersection.

"Get ready," Viktor whispered, feeling the cold heft of the silenced handgun in his hand. It was a beautiful piece of dark machinery—black as midnight, silent as death.

The light ahead turned green. Peter, his attention split between the road ahead and the constant rearview glances, rushed through it.

"This is it," Anton said, his fingers tightening around the steering wheel.

Viktor powered down the window as they drew level with Peter. The gun emerged from the car, a serpent sticking its head out to strike. Peter sensed the movement at the edge of his vision—a sinister glint of black metal.

His fingers grabbed the handbrakes in a chokehold, pulling them toward him with a panic that only the specter of death could induce. His bike jerked, the rear wheel lifting off the ground for a split second.

And in that split second, chaos erupted.

Another car, its driver engrossed in a smartphone, veered into Viktor and Anton's lane. The vehicles collided with a thunderous screech of metal on metal, an abrupt, violent ballet that sent the handgun spiraling from Viktor's grip.

It clattered onto the asphalt and tumbled end over end, finally coming to a rest with a jolt that engaged the trigger. A muted *phut* sounded as the bullet flew, narrowly missing Peter before lodging itself in a telephone pole.

"Fucking idiot!" Anton yelled, stabbing the accelerator as they veered out of the collision. Rubber burned and smoke billowed as they sped away, leaving behind a tableau of twisted metal and frazzled nerves.

Peter's heart was a frenzied drumroll in his chest. His blood roared in his ears, each heartbeat a deafening crescendo in the symphony of his narrowly escaped fate.

He wheeled to a stop, his chest heaving as he looked at the devastation behind him. The other driver was already out of the car, phone still in hand, a mixture of bewilderment and relief splashed across her face.

Had she not been engrossed in her phone, had she not veered off course, Peter knew he would be just another unidentified corpse in a morgue by now. But fate had other plans. And as he sat there, trembling on his bike, he realized that survival was a game of inches and split seconds, a game he was still, miraculously, winning.

But for how much longer?

Peter forced his aching hands to grip the handlebars and propelled himself into motion. He had to get moving, had to disappear, had to live long enough to figure out why his life had suddenly become the fulcrum of a deadly game.

His wheels cut through the streets, a blur of spinning rubber, but in the back of his mind, a voice whispered ominously, insistently.

They know where you are. And next time, you might not be so lucky.

The phrase hung heavy in the air, a pendulum swinging ever closer to the midnight hour of Peter Stroebel's life. And as he rode, a single, gnawing question consumed him.

What happens when the clock strikes twelve?

## SEVENTEEN

The tension inside Lori's office was palpable, as thick and electrifying as the air before a storm. The phone on the desk was like a dormant grenade, ticking away quietly in Cyrillic text messages.

"We need to crack this," Lori said, eyes fixated on the string of indecipherable Russian messages that Shaun had sent to her laptop from the burner phone.

Shaun hovered behind her, peering over her shoulder as she opened a translation website. "Let's make some sense out of this."

With a few swift movements, Lori copied and pasted the Cyrillic text into the translation box. She hit 'Translate', and like some modern-day Rosetta Stone, the site churned the cryptic text into English.

*"Are you safe? Political climate worsening. People are disappearing. We must act now before it's too late."*

*"Have you made contact with the opposition leader? We need to stand against the Kremlin's corruption, replacing our regional leaders like chess pieces!"*

*"We have a solid candidate this time. They can't rig this one. They can't—"*

The translation ended abruptly, a string of distressed emojis taking the place of words.

Lori looked up at Shaun, her eyes a mosaic of shock, intrigue, and urgency. "This isn't just about a rigged election. It's about squashing any opposition—violently, if needed."

Shaun took a deep breath. "Elimination."

Lori massaged the base of her neck, trying to ease the sudden tension that had knotted her muscles. "So the question is, what part does Peter play in all this? Is he opposing the Kremlin?"

"If he is, then that's motive for someone to want him silenced," Lori replied, narrowing her eyes. "This isn't just crooked politics; it's lethal."

Shaun felt a shiver run down his spine, a sense of imminent danger flooding him. "That means it's not just Peter who's in trouble. It could be us too."

Lori sighed. "Yeah, we're not just talking about returning a phone anymore. We're talking about international politics, about covert operations and lives on the line."

The room was charged with the weight of their newfound realization, like a courtroom just before a groundbreaking verdict is announced. Shaun felt his phone buzz. Another call from Russia.

Answering it meant wading deeper into an international quagmire of lethal proportions, but not answering wasn't an option. The boundary between curiosity and responsibility had been crossed.

Shaun pressed the green button. "Hello?"

The response would catapult them into a new realm of peril, the kind they had never encountered in any courtroom.

And so, for Shaun Tolliver and Lori Stetson, the term "due diligence" had just taken on a chilling new meaning: it had become a matter of life and death.

## EIGHTEEN

Peter Stroebel's face was a wet canvas of panic, dripping in rivulets onto the cracked porcelain of the bathroom sink. The cramped room felt more like a trap than a sanctuary. In fact, the entire apartment, a one-bedroom fortress filled with his prized possessions, now seemed like a potential hunting ground.

He splashed another handful of icy water on his flushed face, as though he could wash away the anxiety clawing its way into his mind. As the water trickled down, he took a deep, shuddering breath, feeling the walls close in around him. Every piece of his electric fleet out there on Nashville's streets could be a lure, a shiny hook cast by predatory foes unknown.

His fingers trembled as they turned off the tap, the dripping water seeming to keep time with his racing thoughts. *Who are they? Contract killers? Russian FSB?* The unknown weighed heavy on him, a dark abyss of fear.

His eyes darted to his reflection, searching for a glimpse of the man who thought he could escape, who thought he could stand up to the behemoth that was the Russian system, hidden away in the heart of America. His eyes were like two pools of doubt. The reflection staring back at him wasn't reassuring.

Peter tiptoed across the room, peering through a crack in the curtains that shrouded his living room windows. His heart pounded in his ears as his eyes scanned the nondescript cars parked along the street, the innocent pedestrians walking by. Anyone could be a killer. He was a target dressed up as a common man, and it was getting harder to tell friend from foe.

A droplet of water dangled at the end of his nose, quivering for a moment before plummeting to the hardwood floor below. It splashed, almost unnoticeably, a brief disturbance in a world swirling with chaos.

Suddenly, his business phone buzzed on the counter, the sound tearing through the silence like a bullet. The screen lit up with an incoming call—unknown number. His heart stopped, then revved into overdrive, mimicking the frenetic pulse of his life at the moment.

*To answer or not to answer?* That was the question plaguing him. Answering it could lead him straight into the lion's den; not answering could spell more uncertainty, more shadows lurking in his periphery.

The phone buzzed again, impatient. A second buzz, a third. Each vibration was an ultimatum, a tolling bell urging him to make a decision, and fast.

Peter clenched his fists, took another steadying breath, and reached for the phone.

His finger hovered over the green answer button, a gateway to unknown peril or perhaps, just maybe, a shred of salvation.

He tapped the button. "Hello?"

The voice on the other end would either be a lighthouse guiding him to safety, or the storm that would finally pull him under.

# NINETEEN

The voice at the other end of the line was not what Peter expected—a young-sounding guy, maybe in his early twenties. Certainly not the snarl of an assassin, nor the icy flatness of an FSB agent.

"Are you offering a finder's fee for a bike? My app shows that it's been out of service for a few days and nowhere near the clusters usually get dropped off. I'm new to this charging gig. I have a few scooters I'd like to drop off once they're released," the voice chirped, words dancing with an almost naive enthusiasm.

The blood pounding in Peter's ears seemed to simmer down. It was like an unclenching fist; relief washed over him, albeit cautiously. "Of course, I'll send you the finder's fee if you return it with the scooters when dropping them off."

"The bike is in rough shape and has a flat tire though," said the young man, concern tinting his voice.

Peter felt another wave of relief. "Drop it off anyway, and it will be taken care of."

"Thank you for answering so quickly. I tried other rideshares but found most of them to be rude and always accusing you of hoarding their inventory for finder's fees. This is like my fourth one in two months," the man rambled on.

Curiosity piqued, Peter asked, "How did you get this number, if I might ask?"

"Oh, it's on the website. I can't remember where I saw it, but I dialed it right away," the man replied.

"Alright, thank you. Just drop off the bike and the scooters, and the fee will be transferred to your account."

"Will do, boss!"

Peter ended the call. He stared at the phone for a long moment, the device now inert but fraught with so many implications. On one hand, it was a seemingly harmless call, a simple cog in the machinery of his business. On the other, how could he not doubt? His life was a spider's web of uncertainty; each strand connected to another, each leading to varying degrees of danger.

But for now, there was the business to run—a cover, a lifeline, a ticking time bomb.

Peter's fingers danced over his laptop keyboard as he prepared to transfer the promised finder's fee. Each click was a deliberate movement, each decision a carefully calculated risk.

As he authenticated the transfer, Peter found himself dwelling on the voice from the call. He had sounded sincere, but in a life shaded with subterfuge, where even the simplest exchanges could be veiled threats, sincerity was a luxury he could ill afford.

The finder's fee was sent, the transaction complete. And as Peter closed his laptop, he realized that he'd either just rewarded a good Samaritan or funded the very enemy he was running from.

In this labyrinth of lies, not even good deeds went unpunished.

## TWENTY

Shaun parked his brand-new Audi and pressed the remote lock. The car's headlights blinked twice in affirmation, a mechanical farewell.

"Separation anxiety?" Lori quipped, grinning as she pushed a stray hair behind her ear.

"Funny," Shaun retorted, returning the grin but less convincingly. His mind was already churning through the maze of possibilities that lay ahead.

The pair found themselves walking through the heart of the Slavic community, a foreign tapestry woven into the fabric of America. They were in uncharted territory, yet strangely, they felt a sense of belonging—of shared humanity.

"Our country is amazing, if you think about it," Lori mused, her eyes scanning the shop windows adorned with Cyrillic lettering. "Not just people here, but all over. Different languages, a love for freedom, all under one flag. Most would probably drop their differences with one another if that freedom were threatened."

Shaun looked at Lori, arching an eyebrow. "You thinking about running for mayor or something?"

Lori stopped, her eyes meeting Shaun's. "No, but you can't help but wonder how this all seems to work."

Shaun paused, taking a panoramic mental photograph of their surroundings. Old women haggling over vegetables, children running across the sidewalk playing tag, men chatting fervently in a dialect they couldn't understand. A world within a world. "Even with all the complaints we have at times, it does," he agreed.

As they continued walking, each step echoing their determination, they had no idea they had already been spotted. Across the street, sitting at an alfresco café under the shade of a cobalt-blue umbrella, were Anton and Viktor. Their eyes followed Lori and Shaun with the precision of laser sights.

Viktor's hand hovered over his satellite phone. He looked at Anton, whose eyes were still fixed on the pair.

"Do we engage now?" Viktor whispered in Russian, his hand twitching towards the phone.

Anton looked back at him, considering. "Not yet," he replied, shifting his gaze back to Shaun and Lori. "We need to know how much they know, who else is involved. Any misstep could compromise everything."

Viktor nodded, settling back into his chair, his eyes never leaving the two Americans. He wondered about them, about what made them tick, and what had driven them into this dangerous labyrinth.

Both men knew that the clock was ticking. Soon, the paths of all these lives would converge.

And then there'd be no turning back.

For now, they were all unwitting actors on a grand stage, entangled in a web of geopolitics, personal vendettas, and shifting alliances. As the afternoon sun sank lower, casting long shadows across the bustling streets, everyone had a role to play. And the stakes were life and death.

And so, under the gaze of the Russian spies and amidst the hustle and bustle of a Slavic community stitched into the very fabric of America, Shaun and Lori continued their quest to find Peter.

But in this game of espionage, who was the hunter and who was the hunted?

That was the million-dollar question. And the answer could very well ignite a fire that would consume them all.

## TWENTY-ONE

"Don't look, but I think we're in the right ballpark. Maybe just not the right section," Shaun whispered, his eyes sweeping their surroundings, pretending to be casual. His voice was as low as the sinking sun, but it shot through Lori like a bullet.

"Where?" Lori asked, trying to act nonchalant as she glanced at a shop window filled with Russian dolls.

"Across the street, behind us now. They were sitting at that table with the blue umbrella," Shaun replied, his mind racing faster than his heart.

"You recognized them?" Lori's voice barely concealed her astonishment.

"Tends to happen when people pull out guns and chase you with a complete stranger in the backseat," Shaun retorted, his words tinged with gallows humor.

"Guess so," Lori said, her hands fidgeting. "What's the game plan?"

"Keep walking and see if they follow. If they do, that means they think we're going to meet Peter or are looking for him," Shaun said, his eyes calculating every angle, every escape route.

"How do we know that they haven't killed him already?" Lori questioned, fear creeping into her voice.

Just then, Shaun bent down to tie his shoe, his fingers deftly working the laces as if they were the strings of his fate. Through the reflection on a storefront window, he caught sight of a blur of movement from across the street. It was them. They had abandoned their table under the blue umbrella.

"Because our friends back there are on the move," Shaun said, standing up.

"Following us," Lori concluded, her voice a mix of anxiety and determination.

Shaun nodded. "Exactly. And if they're following us, they don't know where Peter is. That means there's a good chance he's still alive."

They resumed their walk, the pace now subtly quicker. Behind them, Anton and Viktor were closing in, their faces inscrutable masks hiding the danger that lurked within.

It was a treacherous dance on a knife-edge of uncertainty. One false move, one reckless step, and the whole house of cards would come tumbling down, leaving nothing but chaos and regret.

Yet, amid this tension, one thing was clear: For Shaun and Lori, the stakes had never been higher. And their resolve had never been stronger.

In a deadly game of shadows and lies, everyone was committed to their role. The question was, who would be the last one standing?

The air was thick with suspense as they turned a corner, leaving the enigmatic duo of Anton and Viktor to contemplate their next move.

## TWENTY-TWO

Anton and Viktor quickened their pace, their footsteps drumming an ominous rhythm on the concrete. But just as quickly, their steps faltered, slowing in unison like predators sensing a change in the wind. They shared a look. No words were needed; their eyes spoke the language of death.

With a slight nod, they agreed to split up. It was a tactical maneuver, each one taking a side of the street, fanning out like wolves preparing to encircle their prey.

Anton turned left, crossing the street at a brisk pace. His eyes were icy blue glaciers, unwavering and unforgiving. Under his tailored blazer, he felt the weight of his pistol. Attached to its barrel was a silencer—a whisper of darkness ready to extinguish the light.

Viktor remained on the right, mirroring Anton's movements. His eyes, however, were a soul-penetrating black, absorbing everything and revealing nothing. Like his partner, Viktor was armed, a similar pistol-and-silencer ensemble hidden under his own blazer.

As they moved, they carried the air of men who were entirely comfortable being the architects of fate, their fingers mere inches away from pulling the strings that could sever the threads of life.

Anton turned the corner and pressed himself against the brick wall. It was cold, almost as cold as he was. His eyes scanned the horizon, searching for the shape, the shadow, the outline of their prey. Not just any prey, but the specific two who had unwittingly found themselves entangled in a web spun across continents.

Viktor reached the end of his stretch and waited, still as a statue, every muscle primed for action. His eyes never wavered from the path he knew Shaun and Lori would take. A path that would lead them into the jaws of a trap they couldn't yet see.

Unbeknownst to them, Shaun and Lori sensed the tightening noose. With each step, they felt the circle closing in, even though they couldn't quite define its boundaries. They sensed the dread gathering in the air, piling upon each moment like dark clouds foreshadowing a violent storm.

Each pair of eyes—hunter and hunted—searched for the other, their gazes crisscrossing in an invisible battlefield stretched across the streets, searching for that inevitable moment of collision.

It was a deadly dance, choreographed in the hush of twilight, where every step, every glance, every heartbeat could tip the scales in a game where life and death waltzed in a perilous embrace.

## TWENTY-THREE

"They're going to try and cut us off," Shaun said, his voice tinged with a note of urgency that he hadn't intended to let slip.

Lori looked straight ahead, her eyes like two pieces of polished glass trying to reflect only the casual, not the fear lurking behind them. Adrenaline surged through her like electric current, amplifying every sense.

"Suggestions?" she asked, breaking the momentary silence.

"I'm all out at the moment, except for..." Shaun paused, catching sight of something—a glint of hope in an otherwise darkening scenario.

"For what?" Lori pressed, desperate for a lifeline.

"Someone's looking out for us."

As if cued by divine timing, the roar of a motorcycle engine came to life, echoing off the brick facades of the nearby buildings. Rumbling closer was a Nashville police officer on his department motorcycle.

The motorcycle itself was a mechanical beast, a Harley-Davidson decked out in police regalia. Chrome shimmered under the dull glow of the streetlights, contrasting with the matte black of its body. The blue and red lights atop its windshield were dormant but suggested the potential for urgent activity. The leather saddlebags were stamped with the word "Police," as if daring trouble to start something it couldn't finish.

The officer riding the motorcycle was an imposing figure, almost sculpted from stone. His face was stern, weathered by years of witnessing both the best and worst of humanity. His eyes were cloaked behind aviator sunglasses, even in the dimming light, and his uniform was meticulously kept—every badge and insignia shining, his boots polished to a gleaming finish.

"I'll get his attention," Lori said, not waiting for Shaun's agreement. She stepped into the street, flailing her arms like a person signaling a distress signal, her every nerve screaming silently for help.

The officer applied his brakes and the Harley sighed as it came to a stop. He lifted his sunglasses to the top of his head. "Everything alright, ma'am?" His voice was deep and gravelly, like the slow rumble of an approaching storm.

"No, we've seemed to have gotten lost," Lori managed to say, her words carefully measured.

"That's because you typed in the wrong address on your phone," Shaun chimed in, smirking for effect. Lori pulled out her phone and pretended to scrutinize it.

"He's right, my mistake, officer," she admitted, allowing a sigh to escape her lips.

Shaun, meanwhile, scanned the streets they'd just walked. They were empty. Their shadows had vanished into the ether. It was as if they'd never been there at all. But Shaun knew better. Their predatory eyes would be watching from some hidden vantage point, cursing this twist of fate, this thin blue line that had momentarily shielded their intended victims.

"I think we're only a couple of blocks away from the car. We're good, thanks again, officer," Shaun said, finally allowing his tightened muscles to relax, if only a bit.

The officer nodded, lowering his sunglasses back over his watchful eyes. "Stay safe," he warned, as the motorcycle roared back to life and he accelerated away, disappearing down the darkened street like a guardian spirit.

Lori and Shaun exchanged a glance. They knew they'd dodged a bullet, quite literally perhaps. But how long could their luck hold?

As they quickened their pace, each step felt like borrowed time, and the night was far from over.

## TWENTY-FOUR

Viktor and Anton regrouped, their faces showing the strain of professionals challenged. They returned to their table at the café, where the blue umbrella still fluttered lazily in the evening breeze. Cold coffee sat in their cups, abandoned in the urgency of the chase.

"Americans knew we were following them," Viktor said, his eyes narrowing, as if the very acknowledgment pained him.

"Dah," Anton replied, tersely.

There was no need for elaborate conversation. The single syllable carried weight, a universe of concern and complication compressed into one guttural utterance.

"This is going to be a problem we can no longer avoid," Viktor continued, a shade of anger coloring his words. One target had proven vexingly elusive, and it gnawed at him, scratching at the walls of his otherwise ironclad composure.

In Viktor's line of work, uncertainty wasn't an asset; it was a liability that could get you killed. And in America, land of the free, home of the brave, the uncertainties were multiplying. Unlike other parts of the world—places where shadows kept their secrets and the night offered cover—America was full of unpleasant surprises. Traffic cameras. Bystanders with cell phones. Cops on every corner. A minefield of modernity.

Their mission, risky from the outset, was sliding toward the precipice of the unthinkable: failure. They couldn't kill the Americans indiscriminately. A slip-up, even a small one, and they'd set off an international incident, a storm that would ripple across oceans, unsettling the already unstable geopolitical tides.

"It needs to look like an accident," Viktor said, finally, bringing the unspoken into the open.

Anton looked into Viktor's eyes, two pools of icy resolve. For the first time, he allowed himself to consider the prospect of failure, of returning empty-handed. And as quickly as the thought surfaced, he drowned it, suffocated it. Failure was not an option.

The air around them thickened, as if absorbing the gravity of their thoughts, their words. They sipped their cold coffee, a bitter brew that matched their mood. Then, as if synchronized by an invisible conductor, they both rose from their chairs.

The night was still young, and they had work to do. The tightening noose of their mission left no room for mistakes. Their next moves would be calculated with the precision of a grandmaster chess player, each step a critical part of an intricate, deadly ballet.

As they moved away from the café, blending into the folds of the night, one thing was certain: their game was far from over, and their prey had yet to realize the full extent of the danger that hunted them.

## TWENTY-FIVE

Peter Stroebel eased the curtain back into its resting place, his pulse settling into a less frantic rhythm. For a moment, the fabric seemed to hang in the air like a question mark. What next? The scene he'd just witnessed played over and over in his mind, an unyielding loop that refused to be pushed aside.

From his vantage point high above the street, he'd seen Shaun and Lori maneuver their way out of the grasp of their pursuers. Their instinctual response to danger, their survivalist savvy, struck him with a force he hadn't expected. It wasn't just what they'd done; it was how they'd done it. With a finesse, a fluidity, that could only come from a deep-rooted will to live. And then, of course, the cop on the motorcycle. The serendipitous intervention. Was it luck? Destiny? Peter was at a loss.

Luck. That mercurial mistress. She had favored the Americans tonight. But Peter knew not everyone was so fortunate. His mind flicked, like a skipping stone, to his own dire situation. He was a man all too acquainted with the Kremlin's capabilities—those dark arts employed to erase political nuisances.

He felt cornered, encased in a concrete tower that was less a sanctuary than a stage for an impending tragedy. Below him, the streets seemed to seethe with menace, the asphalt and cobblestones circling like predators in a dark ocean, biding their time until he—Peter Stroebel—made his inevitable mistake.

For all the resiliency that had carried him so far, for all the evasive maneuvers and narrow escapes, he knew he was playing a losing game. Playing checkers when the board was set for chess. It was a brutally simple epiphany, but one that rang with the clarity of a struck bell. The men after him weren't just relentless; they were methodical, calculating, each move part of a grander strategy he couldn't yet see.

Peter closed his eyes and took a deep breath, as if drawing courage from the very air. When he opened them, his gaze fell upon a set of chess pieces neatly arranged on a board across the room. The intricate carvings seemed to stare back at him, as though challenging him to rise to the occasion, to change his game.

It was time to move beyond mere survival. Time to engage in a more complex battle of wits and strategy. Time to play chess in a world that didn't afford the luxury of simpler games.

Peter moved to the chessboard, picking up a knight and feeling its weight in his hand. The piece was a warrior, capable of moves that were both linear and lateral. He set it down with resolve.

The rules had changed. And so would he.

## TWENTY-SIX

Viktor's fingers danced over the laptop keyboard with the precision of a concert pianist, his eyes darting from key to screen. Just before they had begun their pursuit, he had snapped a couple of quick and discreet photos of the Americans with his smartphone. A seemingly innocuous action, but one that would set in motion a chain of events, transforming them from shadows to targets. Now, in a hushed cafe teeming with the murmur of foreign dialects, the machine in front of him came alive.

Viktor uploaded the covertly taken photos into the FSB's facial recognition database. The clattering of dishes and the hissing of the espresso machine couldn't drown out the hum of the software springing to life. This wasn't your run-of-the-mill app; it was an intelligence monstrosity born out of a market that catered to regimes who viewed privacy as quaint but utterly expendable.

Within seconds, his screen erupted in a mosaic of images and text. "Got her," Viktor muttered, almost to himself, as Lori Tolliver's face filled his screen. Nashville attorney. A rising star in the legal world. A woman with the kind of reputation that makes people in power nervous: brilliant, unyielding, relentless. Her life's highlight reel played out before him—case victories, interviews, social media snapshots.

Anton, at a neighboring table, looked over the top of his own laptop, his eyes meeting Viktor's. Their unspoken language, honed over years of clandestine operations, needed no words. A brief nod, a flick of the eye, enough to convey volumes. A covert operation funded through a labyrinthine network of shell companies, all evaporating into the accounts of an American financial institution. The irony was almost poetic.

"We have the identity of one of the Americans," Viktor announced, breaking their silent dialogue.

As if on cue, another face flickered onto his screen: Shaun Tolliver. Captured from an old mugshot, but unmistakable. "Now we have the other," Viktor added.

Viktor glanced at Lori's law firm's website. His eyes darted to the address. Downtown Nashville. Less than ten minutes away.

The laptop snapped shut. It was a blink, a momentary lapse in the ceaseless gaze of their operation. But in that blink, the landscape had changed, the storm's path had shifted.

The eye of the storm was closing in, and Viktor and Anton were now its architects.

## TWENTY-SEVEN

Shaun Tolliver's pulse was a drumline in his ears, each beat drowning out the whine of his new Audi's engine. The dashboard's glow painted the car's plush interior with an ethereal light, punctuated by the occasional sweep of headlights from a passing vehicle. His sister, Lori, had always emphasized punctuality. She had stuck her neck out for him when no one else would, offering him a second chance post-parole as the lead investigator at her burgeoning law firm. He had a talent for seeing the invisible, for tracing the forgotten lines that connected facts, people, and motives. Sometimes that meant stepping into the ring with danger—and danger never pulled its punches.

His foot pressed further on the accelerator, coaxing more speed out of the high-performance machine. He had to get downtown, and he was cutting it close. Very close. But just when he thought he might make it, the looming silhouettes of orange barrels emerged ahead like a phalanx of soldiers, funneling the fast-moving traffic into a choking point.

"Damn it," Shaun hissed.

But then, a glimmer of hope—up ahead, an exit ramp opened up like a promised land. If he could just shoot past these last few cars...

The Audi surged forward as if understanding the urgency, the speedometer's needle climbing aggressively. With a flick of the turn signal, Shaun swerved onto the off-ramp. He almost smiled. Almost.

His foot moved to the brake pedal—and met no resistance. It was like stepping into air.

"NO, NO, NO!" He stomped on the brake, his foot plunging down as if through quicksand.

The world outside began to blur, the sharp curve of the exit approaching at an impossible speed. With a sickening lurch, the Audi veered off the asphalt, launching into a terrifying descent down a steep, embankment. The car sliced through a wire fence as if it were made of paper. It became airborne for a second—a heart-stopping, time-stopping second—before crashing into a telephone pole.

The world spun, metal shrieked, and then with a deafening boom, the car skidded into the parking lot of a fast-food restaurant, finally coming to a rest, its front end crumpled grotesquely.

As plumes of smoke billowed from the mangled Audi, Shaun fought to catch his breath, his heart still hammering like a manic drummer in a death metal band. He touched his forehead; his hand came away bloody.

His car—his beautiful new car—was totaled. But as he sat there, trying to comprehend what had just happened, one thought surged above the rest:

He had survived. But why did it feel like he had just dodged an execution?

And somewhere in that tangled maze of thoughts, another chilling question materialized: Was this an accident—or was it something more sinister?

## TWENTY-EIGHT

Lori Tolliver sat behind her broad mahogany desk, cluttered with legal briefs and open case files. Her office was a sanctum of justice, walls adorned with her law degree and various awards that testified to her sharp legal mind and relentless pursuit of justice. The room was permeated with the faint aroma of coffee, emanating from a half-full mug that had been neglected as time had ticked away, each second heavy with the weight of expectation.

Her gaze darted to the vintage wristwatch clasping her wrist—Shaun was late. He had only been late once before, and that was a day he had won the lottery—literally. But today was different; her gut told her so. Worry nibbled at the fringes of her consciousness, each unanswered minute intensifying the feeling.

She picked up her smartphone, its screen void of notifications. With a flick of her thumb, she dialed Shaun's number, waiting for the familiar ring on the other end. Instead, she was met with the digital flatness of his voicemail.

Lori bit her lip. Something was off—she could feel it like a chill up her spine. She was due in court within the hour, a pivotal case teetering in the balance. Her clients were counting on her; her career had been building to moments like this. But now her thoughts were hostage to her brother's inexplicable absence.

The clock on her office wall seemed to mock her, its hands moving in their relentless circuit. She glanced again at her phone; still nothing. A silence loud enough to drown out the world.

She considered her options. Should she go ahead to court and hope that Shaun would catch up? What could've possibly held him back? Traffic? An accident? The questions circled like vultures in her mind.

Lori looked at the clock one more time. She had to make a decision, and she had to make it now. Her next move might solve a puzzle, save a life, or escalate her growing sense of dread into a full-blown crisis.

For the first time in a long time, Lori Tolliver felt torn between her family and her duty. And as the seconds ticked away, she realized that choosing between the two might just be the most difficult cross-examination she'd ever faced.

And then her phone buzzed, a text message flashing on the screen. Her heart caught in her throat as she reached for it.

## TWENTY-NINE

The world tilted, gravity yanking Shaun toward a sudden, merciless meeting with the ground. The jolt was like being punched by the earth itself, a violent kiss that left him reeling. Stars exploded in his vision, tiny supernovas in a field of black.

Blood oozed from a gash on his forehead, the warm fluid sliding down his skin like a river of regret. Sounds were distorted, voices distant as if down a long tunnel, echoing back at him in fragments of broken conversation.

"Can you hear me, sir? What's your name?"

The question floated toward him through the haze. A paramedic's face, young and concerned, hovered in his field of vision, attempting to anchor him to reality. Another paramedic joined, and together they eased him onto a gurney with clinical efficiency.

"Do you know where you are?"

Shaun struggled to form words, his tongue thick and unwieldy in his mouth. The world felt like it was spinning, rotating on an axis that only he could feel. He wanted to speak, to confirm he was still a part of this world, but the effort was herculean.

"Is there anyone we should call? Family? Friends?"

This question pierced the fog. Lori. He needed to get a message to Lori. He felt a sudden surge of urgency, a frantic need to communicate that battled against his disorientation. The paramedic noticed his struggle and moved closer, phone in hand, ready to dial.

But before he could articulate the thought, a wave of nausea crashed over him, dark spots dancing before his eyes like malevolent specters. The grip he had on consciousness was slipping, the world receding as if being sucked away by an unforgiving tide.

And then everything went dark. A deep, consuming darkness that swallowed him whole, pulling him away from the urgent voices, away from the questions, away from the growing sense of impending doom.

## THIRTY

Shaun Tolliver knew pain—had tasted it in a muddy high-school football field under the scrutiny of Friday night lights; had worn it like a second skin in the tangled mess of prison-yard brawls. But this—this was a whole other species of agony. A car accident at breakneck speed had taken his acquaintance with pain and dialed it up to an eleven.

His head was a war zone of conflicting sensations, a battleground where sharp jabs of discomfort clashed with dull, pulsating aches. It felt like his skull was split down the middle, as if someone had performed a botched lobotomy with a blunt instrument.

The room around him was a blur, as if he were viewing the world through a foggy lens. But among the hazy shapes and indistinct colors, he could discern two forms standing at a distance, locked in conversation. Words floated through the air, disjointed and distorted, but one voice broke through the miasma with a crystal clarity.

Lori.

Her voice was the light in the gloom, a beacon guiding him out of the stormy sea of his own disorientation. Though the words she spoke were unclear, her tone—full of concern, tinged with what sounded like relief—was a lifeline.

In this moment, Shaun was aware of two things. The first was that he was immensely, profoundly grateful to be alive. And the second was the piercing realization that something was deeply, irrevocably wrong.

His mind might have been a swirl of clouds and confusion, but the gut instinct that had served him so well through life—on the field, in the yard, in dark alleyways—was ringing loud and clear. And it was telling him this: he was still in the eye of the storm. This was but the briefest respite, the eye in the hurricane, before the winds would pick up again, more ferocious than before.

As his eyes began to focus, the room materializing into sharper relief, Shaun braced himself for whatever lay ahead. It was a feeling he knew well—like lining up for the first snap of a game or squaring off against an opponent. The difference, though, was that this time he didn't know the rules, didn't understand the game that was unfolding around him.

But one thing was for sure: ready or not, the next play was coming, and it was coming fast. And as the medical machinery beeped its incessant, rhythmic chorus around him, Shaun Tolliver girded himself for whatever was about to come barreling his way.

## THIRTY-ONE

Viktor and Anton sat in a sleek, unmarked black sedan, tinted windows providing them with a veil of anonymity. They were parked in an adjacent lot that offered a panoramic view of the chaos that had unfolded on the exit ramp. The crash site was now swarming with flashing red and blue lights, the night air punctuated by the urgency of sirens.

Through the windshield, they watched as paramedics worked fervently around a gurney. Shaun Tolliver lay on it, unresponsive, his face a mask of pain and disorientation. Then the ambulance doors slammed shut, the siren wailed, and the vehicle accelerated into the morning, on its way to whatever destiny had in store for its passenger.

Viktor's eyes, cold as the Arctic Sea, never wavered from the scene. Anton, next to him, was equally focused, his mind already racing through the next steps of their operation.

"Time to move," Viktor finally said, his voice tinged with a guttural edge. He looked at Anton, who merely nodded. They had worked together long enough to communicate almost telepathically.

Viktor exited the car just as a tow truck rumbled onto the scene. Its hydraulics whined as the flatbed tilted downward, ready to hoist the wrecked Audi.

But as the driver prepped his winch and hooks, Viktor approached him. "Excuse me, that's my friend's car. He had some important documents inside. Mind if I take a quick look?"

The tow truck driver, a burly man with grease-streaked overalls, eyed Viktor skeptically. But there was something in the Russian's demeanor, a certain authoritative tone laced with courtesy, that made the driver relent.

"Make it quick," he grunted, stepping aside.

Viktor nodded and moved swiftly. Each step was precise, calculated, as if he were diffusing a bomb rather than rummaging through a car. His eyes fell on the shattered console, the skewed steering wheel, and finally, the battered cellphone on the passenger seat.

A tight smile crossed Viktor's lips. In one fluid motion, he picked up the phone and slipped it into his coat pocket. "Thank you," he said, nodding at the tow truck driver as he exited the wreckage. "There wasn't anything of importance. You can proceed."

As Viktor returned to the car, Anton looked at him questioningly.

"We have his phone," Viktor said, his eyes glinting with a feral excitement. "And soon, we will know if Shaun Tolliver can lead us to Peter Stroebel. After all, a phone can reveal many secrets."

As the black sedan slipped into the traffic and merged into the anonymity of the daylight, both men were acutely aware that their mission had entered a perilous new phase—a phase in which they could no longer afford mistakes, for the stakes were higher than ever.

## THIRTY-TWO

Peter Stroebel stared at his laptop, his icy blue eyes locked onto the news alert scrolling across the top of the screen. The words seemed to blur into each other, but the message was as clear as crystal—*accident involving Shaun Tolliver.*

His cursor hovered over the banner, finally clicking it like a bomb detonator. The screen filled with a news article, complete with pictures of the mangled Audi and a sea of flashing red and blue lights. A chill ran down Peter's spine as he studied the photos. It was as if Lady Luck had fled the scene, leaving behind a twisted pile of metal and despair.

Yet, among the wreckage, there was a glimmer of hope—an image of Shaun being wheeled into an ambulance. His face looked battered but conscious, and that set gears into motion in Peter's mind.

*The burner phone. If Shaun was aware enough, he might know where it is.*

Peter felt like he was hanging by a thread over a chasm of uncertainty, the burner phone being the lifeline that still connected him to some semblance of security. He had to find out.

His fingers flew over the keyboard as he googled the local hospitals. A series of phone calls commenced. Disguising his voice and switching accents like a man wearing different masks, he finally hit gold. "Yes, Mr. Tolliver is here. Room 305. No, he has not been discharged yet," a curt voice from the hospital's front desk offered.

Peter leaned back, absorbing this like a sponge. Every piece of information was a weapon, and he was slowly arming himself.

His eyes darted to the window of his makeshift safehouse, an inconspicuous apartment surrounded by a labyrinth of similar-looking buildings. For all he knew, Viktor and Anton could be anywhere, watching, waiting for him to make that fatal mistake. The accident had proven that they were getting close, maybe too close.

It was time to make a move.

Peter shut his laptop with a decisive click, its sound echoing in the silence like the cocking of a gun. But before he left, his eyes settled on a chessboard sitting at the edge of the table. The black and white pieces seemed to mock him, a reminder of the dangerous game he was caught in.

*Chess, not checkers,* he thought, grabbing his jacket and heading for the door. His next move could very well determine if he was the predator or the prey.

As he exited the room, he knew the pieces were in motion. The only question now was, would it be a checkmate or a stalemate?

And so, like a shadow slipping through the cracks of the evening, Peter Stroebel vanished into the night. His destination: Room 305. His goal: to retrieve his lifeline and possibly, just possibly, turn the tables on his hunters.

## THIRTY-THREE

Peter Stroebel stepped out of the elevator, taking a deep breath. He felt the artificial air fill his lungs, sterile and devoid of life, much like his current situation. He had always been good at blending in, a human chameleon whose survival often depended on being unnoticeable.

His eyes, now hidden behind nondescript reading glasses, scanned the hallway. Nurses walked past, their faces weary but focused. Doctors consulted charts and digital devices. Nobody gave him a second glance. The hospital scrubs he wore were slightly oversized, but they did the trick. The badge swinging from a lanyard around his neck was the cherry on top—no photo, but emblazoned with the hospital's logo and some generic title.

*Infiltration has its charms,* he thought.

The elevator journey had been a serendipitous twist. The gaggle of medical staff who had joined him mid-ride were too engrossed in their own conversations to notice him. But they had sparked an idea, leading him to exit on the floor below Shaun's. The employee lounge had been just as accommodating, offering up a spare set of scrubs and an unattended badge.

As Peter walked down the long, fluorescent-lit corridor toward Room 305, his mind was racing. This was a high-stakes game where the rules were fluid and the players unpredictable. He was treading the razor-thin line between audacity and recklessness, and one wrong move could send him tumbling down an abyss from which there was no escape.

*Just a little further,* he thought, glancing at the room numbers as they increased incrementally.

Finally, he arrived at Room 305. He paused, listening for any sound from within. Silence. He pushed the door open gently, peering inside. Shaun lay on the bed, a maze of tubes and wires snaking around him like electronic vines. His eyes were closed, but his breathing was steady. On a nearby table lay a bouquet of flowers, a Get Well Soon card, and—most crucially—a cellphone.

*There it is,* Peter's eyes narrowed at the sight of the device. *My lifeline.*

In a quick, fluid motion, he closed the distance and grabbed the phone. Slipping it into his pocket, he was about to turn around and make his exit when the door creaked open behind him. His heart leapt into his throat as he spun around to see—

Who was it? A nurse? A family member? Or had his past finally caught up to him in the worst way possible?

It was now or never. His next move would determine if he'd made a masterstroke or a fatal error.

The door swung open fully, and Peter braced himself for what came next.

*Checkmate or stalemate,* he thought. *This is the moment of truth.*

## THIRTY-FOUR

Lori Tolliver's eyes narrowed like a hawk zeroing in on its prey. "What do you think you're doing?" The room seemed to shrink, the tension thickening the air until it was almost unbreathable.

Peter was caught, his gut tightening like a noose. "Put that back, now," Lori demanded, her voice a mix of authority and disbelief.

Shaun's eyes fluttered open, a sheen of pain and confusion coating them. "It's him," he mumbled, his voice soft but unmistakable.

"Our passenger from the other night," Lori pieced it together, her eyes widening but staying trained on Peter. "How did you—"

And then, the dam broke. Peter Stroebel, a man so enigmatic he'd made a life out of shadows, began to unravel. "I saw the news, the accident. You were also followed by the men sent to eliminate me."

Lori glanced at Shaun, her eyes conveying a sea of emotions. "You were right. We were close."

"Close to what?" Shaun tried to sit up but grimaced, clutching his head. "Why are you here in the country?"

Peter's eyes shifted from Lori to Shaun and then down to the phone in his hand. "I tried to make a difference. To change a political system etched in corruption. The populist candidate, our campaign staff..." His voice trailed off, as if carrying a burden too heavy to vocalize.

"The Russian government is trying to kill you? Here, in America?" Lori couldn't believe what she was hearing.

Peter nodded, his face grim. "Sent by the Kremlin, I think."

Shaun groaned, fighting through the pain. "So these guys after you are like trained assassins or something?"

Peter nodded again. "That's correct."

"How did you end up here? In Nashville, of all places?" Lori asked.

"I tried to blend in. To disappear," Peter explained.

"Why not go to our government? The FBI? The CIA?" Lori was full of questions.

Peter sighed, a soul-deep sound that spoke volumes. "I would've, but I don't have papers. Besides, the regime change they're looking for doesn't include the candidate I campaigned for."

Shaun chimed in, "They would've fed you back to the wolves."

"Leaving him no place to go," Lori finished, her eyes meeting Peter's.

Peter raised the burner phone. "This is my only contact with my family. They are also in hiding."

"Here?" Lori's eyes widened.

Peter shook his head. "No, not here."

Just then, a knock echoed through the tense atmosphere, freezing them all. Lori's eyes shot to the door, her attorney's mind racing through a million scenarios.

*Could it be another shadow from Peter's past? The hospital security? Or someone far more deadly?*

"Who is it?" Lori's voice was barely above a whisper, her hand inching toward the phone to dial for help.

The door opened slowly, inch by inch. Everyone in the room held their breath.

## THIRTY-FIVE

The door swung open, revealing a man in dark green scrubs. His clean-shaven face was framed by wavy, silver hair, lending him an air of distinguished experience. Wire-rimmed glasses perched on a nose that had seen many years, many lives pass under its purview. His eyes were a cool shade of blue, like the first hint of dawn, intelligent yet compassionate. The creases at the corners of his mouth and eyes spoke of years dedicated to the unforgiving rigor of medicine. This was Dr. Shazer, the neurologist, and everyone in the room exhaled as if granted a pardon.

"Mr. Tolliver?" Shazer's gaze settled on Shaun.

Shaun nodded. "That's me."

"Good news," Shazer said, the relief almost palpable in the room.

"I can leave?" Shaun's words were tinged with hope.

"We'll discharge you later this afternoon. Only a slight concussion from what I saw on the tests," Shazer informed. "How are you feeling?"

"Like I ran into a brick wall head first," Shaun quipped, attempting to smile despite the residual pain.

Shazer chuckled, a mirthful yet professional sound. "The pain will eventually subside, but you need to take it easy for a few days."

While Lori listened, her thoughts momentarily pacified by Shazer's reassuring diagnosis, she noticed that Peter had vanished, his absence as quiet and enigmatic as his arrival. Her eyes darted to the door, worry knotting her stomach. She stepped into the doorway and glanced both ways down the empty, sterile hallway. No sign of Peter Stroebel. He had evaporated like mist under the sun.

Shazer, catching Lori's eye, appeared puzzled as he prepared to leave the room. "Something that we need to know about?"

"No," Lori said, forcing a smile. The door closed behind Shazer, its latch clicking like the final piece of a puzzle falling into place.

Shaun, still on the bed, gently rubbed his forehead as if to smooth away the layers of confusion and pain. "He'll be back."

"Why do you say that?" Lori looked at her brother, a hint of urgency lining her voice.

Shaun gestured to where Peter had been standing. "The S.I.M card to his phone is back at my apartment. He may have left, but he's tied to us—in ways we're just starting to realize."

Lori felt a shiver run down her spine. Whether they liked it or not, Peter Stroebel had entangled them in a dangerous web, a geopolitical spider's nest with threads reaching as far as the Kremlin.

*And for better or worse,* Lori thought, *we're now all spiders in the same web.*

She glanced again at the door, half-expecting to see it swing open, to see Peter return, his eyes carrying tales of danger and intrigue. But for now, it remained closed—a barrier separating them from answers, from understanding, from life and death itself.

## THIRTY-SIX

The dinging sound of the elevator echoed like a dissonant note in a tension-filled symphony. As the polished metal doors slid apart, Peter's heart skipped a beat. Viktor and Anton, their expressions unreadable, were moving away from the hospital information desk. A security guard was nearby, speaking to a visibly distressed employee. A photograph—grainy but potentially damning—was in the guard's hand.

Peter's pulse quickened. Time seemed to contract, every millisecond weighted with the gravity of decisions that could mean life or death.

The elevator, like a microcosm of the hospital itself, was a nexus of human drama. Several people disembarked, their faces etched with an assortment of emotions—relief, worry, exhaustion. As they moved out, a new set of passengers moved in, each engrossed in their thoughts, faces lit by the sterile gleam of fluorescent lights.

Peter tucked himself into the back corner, near the brushed steel of the elevator's interior. It was cold and unyielding beneath his stolen scrubs, a stark contrast to the warm, palpable tension that began to fill the small space.

The elevator doors started to close, but not quickly enough.

Viktor and Anton stepped inside. A jolt of adrenaline surged through Peter's veins. It was as if the walls themselves had closed in, the air thickening with imminent danger. The men were but a few feet from him, exuding an aura of menace that was almost palpable.

A moment later, the security guard squeezed in just before the doors sealed them all inside this ascending chamber of secrets. The guard was holding the grainy photograph, his eyes scanning the occupants, his mind obviously sifting through scenarios just like everyone else.

Viktor spoke first, his English unnervingly perfect, devoid of accent. "What happened, patient escape?"

The security guard, unaware that he was speaking to the very men who could answer that question all too well, shook his head. "No. Someone swiped some clothing and a badge from one of our employees."

Viktor shook his head, a false mask of civic concern. "What's wrong with people these days?"

"Wish I had the answer to that one," the guard replied, unwittingly standing in front of Anton and Viktor, obstructing their view of the photo, of Peter.

Peter felt his breath catching in his throat. He was invisible yet glaringly exposed, hidden in plain sight. Every sound—the soft rustle of scrubs, the low hum of the elevator, the mechanized voice announcing the floors—amplified the tension coiled tightly in the air.

It was a deadly game of cat and mouse, except the cats were lions, and the mouse was backed into the tightest of corners, one push of a button away from exposure, one blink away from extinction.

Then, finally, the elevator dinged again, announcing its arrival at a floor—any floor, it didn't matter. The doors opened, offering a temporary reprieve, a brief escape from this chamber teetering on the edge of revelation and disaster.

Peter took a split-second to make a decision. He would leave now, dart into the hallway, and lose himself in the hospital's maze-like corridors. But the question lingered—would he be running into freedom or plunging deeper into the jaws of danger?

Either way, he had no choice. He had to move. Now.

And just like that, Peter Stroebel stepped out of the elevator, leaving Viktor, Anton, and the security guard enclosed in a small space, still filled with unspoken secrets, still fraught with questions and suspicions, yet strangely emptier without him.

As the doors closed behind him, Peter thought, *the game isn't over, it has just reached a new level.* And at that moment, it didn't matter who was the hunter and who was the prey. Because in this dangerous, life-altering game, survival was the only rule that counted.

## THIRTY-SEVEN

Peter thought he was in the clear, that he'd managed another impossible escape. But the moment stretched, elongated, like rubber pulled taut just before snapping. His name—uttered with chilling clarity in an FSB-tinted English accent—shattered the illusion. It was like a gunshot in a silent church, piercing and absolute.

He had only paused for a split second, but it was enough. Enough for Viktor and Anton to recognize the mirage for what it was—smoke and mirrors masking a desperate fugitive.

Adrenaline pumping, Peter tore down the corridor, his new scrubs whipping around him like the flag of some fallen nation. Behind him, Viktor and Anton sprinted like wolves after a wounded deer.

A phlebotomist emerged from a patient's room, her cart filled with vials of life's red essence. Peter dodged, narrowly avoiding catastrophe, but Viktor wasn't so lucky. He collided with the cart, spilling tubes and needles, his hip screaming in agony.

But Anton was relentless, his eyes narrow slits of determination.

Peter burst into the stairwell, flinging the door shut behind him. Anton, only a heartbeat later, kicked it open. His eyes darted up, then down, calculating. Peter, who'd clung to the wall above the door frame like a spider in its web, dropped down, putting all his weight into a two-handed shove that sent Anton tumbling backwards down the stairs.

Infuriated, Anton let out a snarl, but Peter was already gone, climbing another flight, blasting through the door, and into the relative safety of the third floor.

He pushed into Shaun Tolliver's room, lungs burning, every cell in his body saturated with lactic acid and fear. Lori looked at him, her eyes twin orbs of astonishment and confusion.

"Told ya he'd be back," Shaun quipped, a grim smile on his face.

"I need your help; they're going to kill me!" Peter gasped.

"Who?" Lori asked, the word hanging in the air, heavy and dark like a storm cloud.

"The same men that followed you. The same men who probably sabotaged your car," Peter said, each word punctuated by a desperate inhalation.

Shaun's headache was a faint echo now, dwarfed by the immediacy of the threat. He began to strip the bedsheets. With a herculean effort, he hurled a chair through the window. Glass exploded outward, and the night air flooded in, filled with the ambient sounds of the city.

Anton stormed in, gun drawn. He saw Shaun and Lori cowering, saw the bedsheet rope leading out the window, and grinned. He was so focused on the window that he never saw it coming: Shaun lunging forward, wrapping another sheet around Anton's neck. With a guttural shout, Shaun lifted him up and then flung him through the window into the open air.

The gun clattered to the floor. Lori grabbed it just as Viktor, limping and seething, appeared in the doorway. The standoff was electrifying—a coiled spring of potential violence.

Then, the security guard burst in. "Drop your weapons!"

Lori quickly explained, her words tripping over each other in her rush to get them out. But the sickening crunch from below, Anton meeting the concrete in a final, fatal encounter, punctuated her narrative more eloquently than any words ever could.

In that moment, all participants in this deadly game understood something crucial—lines had been crossed, lives irrevocably changed, and there was no turning back.

Everyone in the room felt it, an intangible shift, as if the very air had thickened, become charged. The next moves would be decisive, the stakes irrevocably high, and for better or worse, their fates were now intricately, irrevocably intertwined.

## THIRTY-EIGHT

The room had become a crucible of tension, each soul inside it caught in a gravitational pull toward an unavoidable fate. The security guard's eyes met Viktor's—the former filled with determination, the latter with a cold, predatory emptiness.

Time seemed to slow as Viktor squeezed the trigger. The room echoed with a single, sharp report—a metallic cry that shattered the uneasy silence. The bullet tore through the air, a lethal messenger, and found its mark between the security guard's eyes. For a microsecond, his expression registered surprise, then nothing at all. His body seemed to float before it collapsed to the floor.

Lori's finger jerked on the trigger in raw panic. She had never been comfortable with guns, her aim guided more by emotion than skill. Bullets shredded curtains, obliterated tiles, tore through drywall. In the chaos, Viktor, limping but lethal, vanished into the hallway, a smattering of blood left in his wake.

The room had transformed into a war zone in mere seconds. Plaster dust hung in the air like fog, the acrid smell of gunpowder stinging their nostrils. The piercing wail of sirens approached from outside, and there was a rising clamor of medical personnel gathering around what was left of Anton—grotesquely twisted and undeniably dead.

And then, Peter Stroebel stepped out from the bathroom. His face was ashen, eyes wide, visibly shaking from the cacophony of violence that had just unfolded.

"You said they were after you, not that they'd start a goddamn war in a hospital!" Shaun yelled, his voice cracking from both outrage and the physical toll of the night.

Peter's eyes met Shaun's. "I underestimated them. I underestimated how far they'd go to erase me."

"You think?!" Lori spat, her face flushed with fear and anger. She looked at the gun in her hands as if seeing it for the first time, then placed it carefully on the bed.

Peter moved toward the window, peering cautiously through the shattered glass. Flashing red and blue lights painted the exterior of the hospital. "We need to go, now. Before the place is swarming with police and whoever else Viktor brings."

Shaun struggled to his feet, fighting back a wave of dizziness. "You're talking about running away?"

"Unless you want to be caught in the crossfire when they return, yes, I'm talking about running away," Peter replied, his tone urgent but even.

Lori looked from Shaun to Peter, her mind racing. "I have an idea. But we're going to need a few things."

Peter met her gaze, his eyes filled with a mix of desperation and hope. "Tell me."

As Lori began to outline her plan, each knew that the path ahead was fraught with peril, each turn a dance with danger. The stakes couldn't be higher: a deadly international conspiracy had come to their doorstep, transforming a hospital room in Nashville into ground zero.

## THIRTY-NINE

Viktor stood in front of a dirty, smudged mirror in a dimly lit motel room that smelled of mildew and stale cigarettes. The fluorescent light overhead flickered intermittently, casting ghastly shadows on his face. It was the kind of place you'd find at the fringes of civilization, a haven for those who are running from something—or someone.

His cold eyes, unyielding like steel, scanned his own reflection as he pulled back the makeshift bandage he'd fashioned from a motel towel. The bullet had grazed the fleshy part of his upper arm, a gory streak torn through the skin. The wound was still oozing, crimson rivulets streaming down to his forearm.

He clenched his jaw as he turned the tap, sending a torrent of cold water into the sink. Blood swirled away, tainting the water a delicate, almost ethereal pink. With his good arm, he took another towel, soaked it, and then clenched his teeth as he pressed it against the searing wound. Pain roared through him, hot and sharp, but his eyes remained dead calm. Pain was a companion he'd known for years.

Viktor's phone buzzed on the bedside table next to a tarnished lamp. A message. From Moscow. *Status?*

His thumb hovered over the screen. What was there to say? That he had lost Anton, his trusted comrade? That they had underestimated their prey? That they were now in a perilous game with American civilians? Civilians who had thrown one of their own from a window?

The clock was ticking. Not just in this sordid motel room, but on an international scale. Moscow was losing patience. And once Anton's body was discovered and identified, their quiet operation would evolve into an international scandal. The CIA, the FBI, Interpol—they'd all be scrambling, hunting.

So it was time to change tactics.

His fingers danced over the screen, typing a terse reply: *Complications. Escalating measures.*

Viktor knew that "escalating measures" would set things into motion—actions that would make him either the hunter or the hunted. His arm throbbed in protest as he began to search through his bag, pulling out a syringe and a vial of liquid. It was a paralytic agent; quick, deadly, untraceable in a post-mortem. He wouldn't underestimate Peter Stroebel again, nor would he take chances with the Tollivers.

He carefully loaded the syringe, his eyes never leaving his reflection. In that mirror, he saw not just his own battle-scarred countenance but the grim visages of those who had stood against him over the years. A litany of faces, all gone. All silenced.

In that moment, he was no longer merely an agent, he was a manifestation of fate itself. A wounded predator, yes, but predators are most dangerous when cornered. And as his cold eyes met his own icy gaze, a slow, terrifying smile crept onto his lips.

Peter Stroebel had been clever, but Viktor had been trained by a system far older and colder than anything Stroebel could fathom. It was a game, a deadly game. And Viktor was far from playing his final hand.

# FORTY

Nashville International Airport buzzed with life, a hive of human activity. The overhead announcements echoed in waves, mingling with the chorus of chattering travelers, screaming children, and the relentless hustle of wheeled suitcases over polished floors. The scent of coffee and fast food mingled in the air, conflicting yet oddly harmonious—a testament to the amalgamation of lives and stories momentarily intersecting in this transient space.

Shaun, Lori, and Peter sat in a row of seats near their gate, their nerves strung tighter than the strings of a vintage Gibson guitar. They were all too aware of the unseen predator lurking somewhere in the vicinity. The airport was big enough to lose oneself but not so big that it provided any sense of safety.

Lori checked her phone one more time, her eyes darting to the digital map that showed Shaun's phone moving in the complex web of hallways and terminals. "He's here somewhere," she whispered, her voice laced with apprehension.

Peter's eyes darted nervously before standing. "I have to use the lavatory," he muttered, rising and leaving his baggage behind.

From his vantage point, seated at a coffee shop several gates down, Viktor watched Peter make his move. His eyes narrowed as he placed the cap on his coffee cup. In his pocket, the syringe filled with paralytic felt like a cold promise. He rose to his feet, a predator silently closing in on his prey.

Peter stood before the mirror in the lavatory, staring at his own harried reflection. His hands clenched and unclenched as he tried to shake off the tension. And then the door swung open. In the mirror, he saw Viktor. His heart froze, then raced. Viktor's eyes met his, a chilling smile crept onto his lips.

There was nowhere to go.

Peter retreated into a stall, latching the door shut. Viktor's footsteps echoed ominously on the tile floor. Slow. Methodical. A predator savoring the moment before the kill.

Just as Viktor reached into his pocket, the first stall door burst open. A hulking figure in a dark suit pointed a gun at Viktor. "Federal agents! Drop what you're holding!"

The lavatory entrance exploded with activity. More figures poured in, brandishing weapons that made the first agent's look like a toy. Each step was a cacophony, drowning out the less discernible sounds of the airport.

Viktor's face twisted in a snarl. His eyes, those ice-cold orbs, met Peter's for one last moment. Then, with a speed that defied his size, he stabbed the needle into his own arm and depressed the plunger.

Within seconds, he crumpled to the floor, defeated not by his enemies, but by his own hand. It was over. Viktor would rather die than be captured, than be the fulcrum of an international scandal.

In that lavatory, the scent of disinfectant mingled with the acrid odor of sweat and fear. Agents rushed to Viktor's body while Peter stood frozen in his stall, the gravity of his narrow escape weighing down on him like an anchor.

Back in the waiting area, Lori's phone buzzed with an alert. She looked down, her face a mask of confusion, then relief. Shaun and Lori looked at each other, the unspoken understanding settling between them.

"He's gone," Lori said softly, still not sure whether to feel relief or a lingering, unsettling dread. "Viktor is gone."

And in that bustling Nashville International Airport, teeming with life yet indifferent to the individual dramas unfolding within its walls, three souls sat, intertwined by the fickle threads of fate, forever changed.

The overhead speakers blared, announcing the final boarding call for their flight.

# EPILOGUE

High above the American heartland, a passenger jet sliced through the azure sky like a hot knife through butter. Clouds scattered in its wake, ethereal wisps of water vapor that seemed almost dreamlike in their quiet beauty. But inside the metal tube hurtling through the atmosphere, dreams were being replaced by stark realities.

Peter Stroebel sat next to Lori Tolliver, each wrapped in their own cocoon of thoughts yet inexplicably tethered together by a series of life-altering events. Lori's laptop screen glowed softly, the stark form of an I-589 application displayed in cold black-and-white. Her fingers danced over the keys, filling in the blanks of a document that might determine the fate of the man beside her.

Peter watched as Lori worked, her concentration absolute. The form before her was more than mere bureaucracy; it was a lifeline, a parchment of sanctuary. They were set to meet an immigration attorney the minute they landed in Washington D.C., the nation's power center, where destinies were made and shattered with the stroke of a pen.

As Lori entered the final details, Peter's burner phone buzzed softly. With his SIM card back in place, messages had begun to pour in. He swiped through them, pausing at the texts from his family. Safe. For now, they were safe.

The jet engines hummed a relentless, lulling drone that seemed almost discordant with the pulse-pounding events of the past days. A pact had been formed, an alliance between intelligence communities, Peter, and those who had become unintentionally embroiled in his life. Information for asylum—a quid pro quo as old as time, yet one that had never felt quite so personal.

Lori finally clicked the 'Save' button and closed her laptop, her gaze meeting Peter's. "This is it," she said softly, as though afraid to break the spell that had befallen them since their meeting.

"Yeah," Peter murmured, his eyes clouded with a mix of relief and uncertainty. "This is it."

As the airplane began its descent into the politically charged atmosphere of Washington D.C., the future remained an uncertain expanse, shrouded in mist. But for the moment, inside the belly of the jet, encased in a shell of aluminum and hope, Peter Stroebel and Lori Tolliver flew toward it together.

In that confined space, hurtling toward destiny, two souls found themselves on the edge of a new chapter, their fates written in the ink of courage, resilience, and a series of extraordinary events. They were flying into a future that was anything but certain, but they were doing it with eyes wide open.

And in that final, suspended moment, as the wheels of the jet touched the tarmac, as the passengers braced for the familiar jolt of arrival, it became suddenly, stunningly clear: They had landed.

## More cole steele books:

Nashville justice series

Roman lee series

Willow darby series

ARTIFACT

***Be sure to visit***

***www.colesteele.com[1] for exclusive content and updates***

---

# Don't miss out!

Visit the website below and you can sign up to receive emails whenever Cole Steele publishes a new book. There's no charge and no obligation.

https://books2read.com/r/B-A-AHTI-CZRNC

**BOOKS 2 READ**

Connecting independent readers to independent writers.

# Also by Cole Steele

**Nashville Justice**
Dose of Deception
Silent Strings
Last Call
Client
Miranda
Asylum
Fatal Verse
King of Strings
Ledger

**Roman Lee**
Beneath Devil's Lake
Crimson Rows
Brethren of Liberty
Chameleon
Line Break

**Willow Darby**
Admission

Encounter
Parlay
Departure
Prospectus
Peril
Vesper
Reticle


**Standalone**
Artifact



Watch for more at https://www.facebook.com/authorColeSteele.

# About the Author

Cole Steele is a versatile and talented author residing in the United States. With a vivid imagination and a knack for storytelling, Cole Steele has successfully created two enthralling book stories and a captivating short story series. Cole Steele is deeply grateful to the writers who first ignited the passion for storytelling and provided the inspiration to embark on this creative journey.

With a commitment to crafting immersive worlds and compelling characters, Cole Steele is delighted to offer readers an escape from the mundane and a chance to embark on exhilarating adventures. The warm reception and love for the characters created by Cole Steele have been both rewarding and motivating.

Cole Steele sincerely hopes that you, too, will join the growing community of readers and find solace, excitement, and inspiration in the characters' journeys. So, prepare to dive into the pages and lose yourself in the enthralling worlds that await you.

Read more at https://realcolesteele.wordpress.com/.

9 798223 913474

# The Engl Civil War *in* WESSEX

## CONTENTS

WESSEX BOOKS

# The Siege of Portsmouth

## *Much playing of the ordinance*

**To safeguard the port and military stores as being 'of great consideration to the peace and quiet of this our Kingdom.'**

*Lord George Goring*

Two months before the Civil War officially began, King Charles 1st sent orders from his court at York to the Governor of Portsmouth, Colonel George Goring, to safeguard the port and military stores as being 'of great consideration to the peace and quiet of this our Kingdom.' Portsmouth was vital to the Royalist cause as the King had lost control of the navy and the City of London before even a shot had been fired. Goring declared prematurely for Charles on 2 August before there was any chance of reinforcements. He paraded his garrison of 300 and summoned those within the town who could bear arms, offering them reward if they would 'serve His Majesty in this business.' A contemporary wrote 'some of the soldiers gave a great shout, the rest were discontented'; most leading citizens being for Parliament.

Parliament reacted swiftly, and ordered their Lord General, the Earl of Essex to raise forces and if Goring refused surrender, 'to lay siege against the town and suppress all that shall come to oppose them'. Local Parliamentarian supporters, drawn from the 'gentry and commonality of Hampshire', soon blockaded the landward side of Portsea Island.

On 8 August, Parliamentary warships sailed into the Solent, blockading the harbour mouth and landing armed seamen to secure the Isle of Wight. The following night, a raiding party under Captain Brown Bushall,

*English Sailor of the 1640s*

*Southsea Castle*

rowed into Portsmouth Harbour and seized Goring's only warship, the 6-gun pinnace Henrietta Maria, which was taken without a struggle and sailed across to Fareham Creek. The following day, sailors helped civilian refugees and their cattle to escape from Portsea across Langstone Harbour to safety.

*Sir Williams Waller's Cornet*

The loss of the Henrietta Maria was a blow to Goring's garrison, which was compounded when regular troops arrived from London, joining with the local levies on Portsdown Hill. Commanded by Sir William Waller and Sir John Meldrum, veterans of the Thirty Years War, these reinforcements consisted of two troops of horse (120 men), and 500 foot soldiers drawn from Merrick's Regiment.

Waller's first success was the taking of the little fortification which defended the Portsbridge, the only dry route onto Portsea Island. Several days of skirmishing followed with 'much playing of the ordinance' from the town. Despite messages from the King that help was coming, the garrison began to shrink, and when they saw that across the water at Gosport there was 'much digging with pickaxes', showing that the enemy was constructing a battery, 'they were much troubled'. In vain Waller attempted to persuade Goring to surrender, and with the completion of the Gosport battery on 2 September, Portsmouth came for the first time under heavy bombardment. The following night, Waller captured, without loss, Goring's outpost at Southsea Castle, the Governor, Captain Challenor, being drunk. This unexpected defeat so undermined Goring's men that, next morning, it was unanimously agreed to treat for surrender. Waller granted generous terms and on 7 September, the siege ended, and that evening 'Colonel Goring took boat and rowed unto ship for Holland'.

*The Round Tower and Square Tower Part of Portsmouth's Fortifications*

# The Battle for Babylon Hill

## A hill of confusion

**Hartford, failing to raise Wiltshire, tried in Somerset.**

**Hartford withdrew to Sherborne in Dorset.**

*Marquis of Hartford*

On 2 August, William, Marquis of Hartford was commissioned by King Charles to be Lieutenant General of the six Western Counties. Chosen for his social standing rather than military skill, Hartford was fortunate to have the services of Sir Ralph Hopton who had soldiered on the continent. Hartford, failing to raise Wiltshire, tried in Somerset, moving his HQ to the Bishop's Palace at Wells. The Somerset gentry however were for Parliament, raising vastly superior numbers of men with which on 5 August they appeared on the hills around Wells. Hartford barricaded the roads but was greatly outnumbered and the Palace came under artillery fire. Next morning Hartford withdrew to Sherborne in Dorset, where the pro-Royalist Digby family owned the Old Castle. Partly surrounded by a shallow lake, the castle stood at the eastern end of the town. Here Hartford quartered his soldiers whilst making the old fortification defensible again.

Hartford and Hopton gathered 400 infantry, 60 dragoons armed with sporting guns and several troops of horse and gentlemen volunteers. On 2 September, the Parliamentarian Earl of Bedford approached, with a force of 7,000. Hopton skirmished with Bedford's advance guard so successfully that the Earl's troops did not enter Sherborne, camping north of the castle, where they set up their cannon too far from the castle to do much damage. Hopton's musketeers harassed the Parliamentarian camp so effectively that the morale of the Earl's soldiers plummeted and they began to desert. The next night, Hopton moved his two small cannon and fired into the camp, panicking

*Bishop's Palace, Wells*

Bedford's shrinking army. After two chaotic days Bedford was forced to withdraw to Yeovil. On 7 September, Hopton attempted to attack the new Parliamentary quarters, but he found the River Yeo bridge defended, so drew up his force on the slopes of Babylon Hill, and began long-range fire into Yeovil. Two steep lanes climbed the hill and on these Hopton placed guards, but as the day passed and the enemy made no movement he began to withdraw. For once, Hopton had underestimated his enemy; as he began to move back he was surprised by three troops of Parliamentary cavalry which had secretly crossed the Yeo and used the two now unguarded lanes to reach the summit. Following fierce fighting, Bedford's troops gained the advantage, only nightfall saving Hopton's men. Despite this success, the next day, Bedford retreated back into Somerset.

*Earl of Bedford*

Hartford remained at the castle but reports came in of the surrender of Portsmouth and of the movements of Essex's army in the midlands, cutting off any help from the King.

Hartford's Council of War decided to abandon Sherborne and march to Royalist South Wales, using coal boats from Minehead to cross the Bristol Channel. Hopton reluctantly agreed, and they reached Minehead on 22 September, to find just two ships and Bedford's cavalry closing on their rear. Hartford sailed for Wales with the foot and baggage, whilst Hopton with 200 horse and dragoons rode west into Cornwall to form a new army.

*Remains of Hanger Sword found at Babylon Hill*

*View of Babylon Hill*

# The Battle of Lansdown

## 5 July 1643

### As unmoveable as a rock

**The King ended the year in Oxford which became the Royalist HQ for the rest of the war.**

**The Royalists crossed the Avon intending to occupy the commanding ridge at Lansdown.**

Bedford rejoined the main army, serving under the Earl of Essex at the inconclusive battle of Edgehill. The King, having made an abortive attempt on London, ended the year in Oxford which became the Royalist HQ for the rest of the war. Diplomatic efforts to bring about peace during the winter failed, and before spring, military operations began again. Essex captured Reading in April but typhus stalled his army's advance.

In the meantime, the west was succumbing to Royalist pressure thanks mainly to the efforts of Hopton who had built a formidable army in Cornwall, backed by local Royalist gentry headed by Sir Bevil Grenville. As the Cornish army was mostly infantry, the King sent Hartford and Prince Maurice with cavalry to reinforce them. The two forces rendezvoused at Chard in June, bringing Hopton's strength up to 7,000 men. Opposing Hopton was Sir William Waller with a similar sized force but with more cavalry, and fewer infantry. Falling back to Bath to halt the Royalists amongst the steep terrain, Waller was joined by Sir Arthur Haselrig's regiment of 'prodigiously armed' heavy cavalry known as the 'lobsters'.

On 4 July 1643, the Royalists crossed the Avon and marched to the east of Bath, outflanking Waller's strong position at Claverton Down, intending next morning to occupy the commanding ridge at Lansdown. Waller however, anticipated this, and occupied the ridge himself before daylight, constructing earthworks to emplace his artillery. Hopton arrayed his army on Toghill, north of Lansdown and separated from it

*Lansdown Hill*

by a deep valley. Parliamentary cavalry skirmished with the Royalist advance guards, but it was obvious to Hopton that Waller would not be tempted from his strong position, so he decided to continue on his march to join the King at Oxford. Seeing the enemy withdrawing, Waller sent 1,000 cavalry and dragoons to charge them in the flank and rear, causing utter confusion in the narrow lanes. Fortunately for Hopton, his musketeers made a stand allowing his cavalry to regroup and push the Parliamentarians back.

*Sir Bevil Grenville*

Hopton agreed on an assault and sent his main body up the steep lane in the centre, with musketeers sweeping round on the flank. Three times the assault went in, only to be repulsed each time, and so demoralising the Royalist cavalry that half of them fled. Eventually Sir Bevil Grenville, at the head of his pikemen, made one last effort and stormed the ridge, costing him his own life. There 'they stood as upon the eaves of a house for steepness, but as unmoveable as a rock'.

Waller's army withdrew behind a still-existing field wall to the south of the battlefield, but both sides were too exhausted to continue. Under cover of darkness, Waller withdrew to Bath with his army still intact.

*Sir William Waller*

Morning saw the Royalists still in possession of the field, but at great cost. This was compounded when a powder wagon blew up next to Hopton, temporarily blinding him. Much weakened, and with Waller hot on their tail, they limped towards Oxford.

*Civil War Dragoon*

*Grenville Monument*

# The Battle of Roundway Down

## 13 July 1643

*Great William the Con – so fast did he run*

**Waller unsuccessfully tried to storm the town; evidence of his cannonade is still visible on St John's and St James's churches.**

Hopton's army reached the shelter of Devizes on the evening of 9 July thanks to a costly rearguard action fought at Rowde Ford north-west of the town. That night the Royalists held a Council of War at the injured Hopton's billet deciding that Hartford and Maurice should break out with the cavalry towards Oxford whilst Hopton would hold Devizes until relieved. The escaped cavalry arrived, exhausted, in Oxford the morning of 11 July.

The King had made efforts to succour his western army; sending first Lord Crawford with ammunition and 600 cavalry from Oxford on 9 July, and then Lord Wilmot with his brigade of horse. With the arrival of Maurice's weary men, those that could still ride were given fresh mounts and joined with Sir John Bryon's brigade also going to the relief of Devizes. Hopton's men meanwhile were making use of hedges and barricades to defend the place. Waller unsuccessfully tried to storm the town; evidence of his cannonade is still visible on the

*Cuirassier*

*Civil War damage, St John's Church, Devizes*

St John's and St James's churches. On the night of 11/12 July, Waller's cavalry surprised Crawford's approaching convoy, capturing much of the ammunition. With this success he tried to persuade the Royalists to discuss surrender terms. Hopton had no intention of capitulating but prolonged negotiations to gain time for the relief force which had rendezvoused at Marlborough. The morning of 13 July Waller had news of the advancing Royalists, so drew up his army of 2,000 horse, over 2,000 foot and seven guns on the chalk down to the north-east of Devizes called Roundway, facing the Marlborough road. Below them was a large open plateau enclosed by 'four hills, like four corners of a die'. Onto this plateau, through a gap in the ancient Wansdyke, filed Lord Wilmot with 1,800 Royalist cavalry. Wilmot had two cannon fired to warn Hopton that he had arrived and would need the support of his infantry. Initially the Devizes Royalists, suspecting a trap, stayed put.

*Lord Wilmot*

Waller deployed his army with foot in the centre, flanked by his horse, the right wing consisting of Haselrig's heavy cavalry. Wilmot likewise arrayed his forces in three brigades. It appears that Waller made the first move, by sending forward Haselrig's wing, hoping to dispose of Wilmot before Hopton could join in. The Royalist horse had a much broader front and enveloped their tightly packed opponents and drove them from the field. Waller's left wing was similarly defeated and sent crashing over the down at 'Bloody Ditch'. The exposed Parliamentary infantry started to withdraw in good order, but soon came under attack, and with the eventual appearance of Hopton's troops, they began to run.

*Sir Ralph Hopton*

Following this most complete of victories, Hopton's forces marched north and joined the King's army under Prince Rupert at the successful storm of Bristol, on 26 July. These combined forces then marched on Gloucester expecting it to surrender. However when the King appeared before the city on 10 August, he was met with a defiant refusal.

*Roundway Down*

# The Battle of Aldbourne Chase

## 18 September 1643

*To charge their horses in flank*

**Essex reached Swindon, whilst 10 miles to the east, the King's army camped at Alvescot.**

Gloucester's resistance was a turning point of the war; rejuvenating the Parliamentary cause. Essex's army, languishing in the Thames Valley, was reinforced with troops from London and set out to relieve the beleaguered city which he did on 5 September, the King having withdrawn to Sudely.

Charles planned to intercept Essex on his return to London but did not know which route he might take. Essex bluffed the King by advancing to Tewkesbury where his engineers constructed a bridge of boats across the Severn as if he intended to march on Hereford. The King ordered his army to Pershore to block the route to London, but Essex wrong-footed him by leaving Tewkesbury on 15 September, and heading south-east. That night, Essex's advance guard surprised two regiments of Royalist horse asleep in Cirencester and captured 40 wagonloads of much needed food. When this news reached the King he set out in pursuit.

On Sunday 17 September, Essex reached Swindon, whilst 10 miles to the east, the King's army camped at Alvescot.

It was obvious to the King that Essex was making for the Great West Road so he planned to block this route at Newbury if he could get there first. To do this he detached his nephew Prince Rupert with a force of 5-6,000 horse to harry and slow the enemy.

On 18 September, Essex's army began the climb up onto the Marlborough Downs intending to billet at Hungerford. The army had almost crossed the great open

*Cavalry trooper*

*Civil War re-enactment in Aldbourne Close*

10

space of Aldbourne Chase when Prince Rupert's 1,000 strong advance guard under Colonel Urrey fell on the small rearguard under Colonel John Middleton. Simultaneously Rupert and the main body of the Royalist horse appeared on the flank of Essex's army, which was in line of march. Middleton's men were pushed back to the main body of the army but managed to regroup and cover the infantry whilst they marched on towards Aldbourne. The Royalists attacked again but Middleton counter-charged and put them in disorder until their greater numbers halted him.

Assisted by a small party of musketeers from Essex's regiment, more Parliamentary cavalry joined the action but they too were forced back to the main army. Rupert had done what was required, and with the approach of darkness withdrew his men. In the night, Essex's army limped through Aldbourne to Hungerford to rest the next day.

On Tuesday, Essex marched for Newbury, his left flank was covered by the River Kennet (at this time the London road ran south of the river). His quartermasters rode ahead to procure provisions and quarters for the army in the town. They arrived in late afternoon but were soon surprised by Royalist cavalry who quickly overwhelmed them. Newbury had fallen, the King had won the race, but the next day, Essex successfully battered his way through and Charles, short of ammunition, withdrew to Oxford for the winter. For Charles, it was his last real chance of winning the war in a single action.

*Robert Devereux, Earl of Essex*

*Prince Rupert*

*Troop Cornet, Earl of Essex's Regiment*

# The Storming of Alton

## December 1643

*Here grew a very hot fight*

**Attacking from the north against a strong earthwork and a brick building.**

That summer, the Royalists seized most of Wessex except for the isolated garrisons at Lyme Regis, Poole, Southampton, Portsmouth and Wardour Castle. Hopton, recovered from his wounds, was given command of a new army. In the meantime, Waller also had a new army, which included three regiments of the London Trained Bands, to defend the Southern Counties. He set out to attack Royalist Basing House, but bad November weather forced him to lift the siege and with the imminent arrival of Hopton he withdrew to Farnham Castle. Hopton pursued but found Waller's position too strong, so instead, marched into Sussex taking Arundel Castle on 9 December. To cover Waller he left behind in Odiham 900 infantry and a force of cavalry and dragoons under Lord Crawford, who, finding difficulties in obtaining supplies drew into winter quarters in Alton.

Waller assembled his force of 5,000 men at 7pm on 12 December on a heath outside Farnham and began a bogus march on Basing House. At 1am, Waller altered his line of march to the south and arrived to the north-west of Alton. Lord Crawford, taken by surprise, managed to escape with the cavalry but Waller's horse quickly surrounded the town to prevent the infantry escaping. Waller's infantry were divided into three divisions, the first attacking from the north against a strong earthwork and a brick building. Here the Royalists had positioned most of their musketeers who poured heavy fire from the windows.

*Trained Band soldier*

*Pair of leather guns in the West Highland Museum*

*Roundshot (35mm) from leather gun from Alton churchyard*

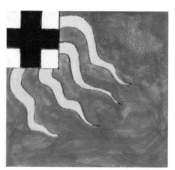

*London Trained Band, Westminster Auxileries Colour*

They were eventually dislodged when Waller deployed his train of artillery, consisting of a number of 'leather guns', light-weight, portable pieces newly received from London. The Royalists fell back to the churchyard of St Lawrence's. The London Brigade stormed another earthwork and with colours flying and shouting their field-word of the day 'Truth and Victory', advanced towards the church.

St Lawrence's was surrounded by a stone wall and flanked by a barn, which the Royalists took advantage of as defences. A two-hour fire fight ensued, smoke from a burning building adding to the confusion. Eventually a number of the defenders fled, but it was some time before the Parliamentarians realised they had gone. Then they poured in. The defenders, finding that the enemy were in the yard, ran in confusion to the church, its door choked with fleeing men. Waller's troops threw grenades through the windows before entering the church where the Royalists made a last stand behind a barrier of dead horses. Colonel Bolles led the defence, crying 'God damn his soul if he did not run his sword through the heart of him which first called for quarter'. Bolles was eventually killed, and with his death the Royalists surrendered. Over 800 were taken, 'coupled together and brought to Farnham'. To Hopton, the loss of these men was 'as a wound that will not heal'.

Hopton was to endure another loss, for on 6 January, Arundel was forced to surrender to Waller because of lack of supplies. Snow then put paid to any serious campaigning until spring.

*Battle damaged door, St Lawrence's Church, Alton*

*St Lawrence's Church, Alton*

# The Siege of Wardour Castle

## *We heard a noise of digging*

**This tower house had been captured by Sir Edmund Hungerford from Lady Blanche Arundell.**

Whilst campaigns were fought through Wessex, the garrison of Wardour Castle in south Wiltshire had been away from the main action. This tower house, the home of the Royalist and Catholic Arundell family, had in the spring of 1643, been captured by local Parliamentary commander Sir Edmund Hungerford from Lady Blanche Arundell and a small garrison following a siege of six days.

Although damaged, Parliament decided that the castle should not be destroyed but re-garrisoned. Major Edmund Ludlow was chosen to be its new governor with Captain Bean's company of foot to man it.

Republican Ludlow had served with Essex's Lifeguard before being sent west to reinforce the Parliamentarian cause. After a fortnight, Lord Arundell came against the damaged castle with a detachment of cavalry to demand surrender. Ludlow refused, and being without support Arundell withdrew without firing a shot. Ludlow assumed he would not be undistured for long, and brought in provisions and

*Edmund Ludlow's Cornet*

*Old Wardour Castle*

ammunition from Southampton, paid for by the discovery of over £1,200 hidden in the castle.

As Parliamentary fortunes began to wane in the west, Wardour became more and more isolated, and Ludlow was given orders that if the situation worsened he could slight the castle and withdraw. This was not an option that the determined Ludlow was going to take.

That summer, Wardour appeared to be left alone by the Royalists, which enabled Ludlow to strengthen his defences. But he was not forgotten. A boy of twelve was bribed by the Royalists to obtain a post within the kitchen, from whence he was secretly to 'poison' the castle's artillery. He had sabotaged a 'wall gun' on the tower roof before being apprehended. He had done this by introducing acid into the barrel of the gun which caused it to burst when fired. It is not recorded what happened to the boy.

*Edmund Ludlow*

In December the Royalists, under Captain Bowyer lay siege to the castle. Bowyer constructed an earthwork to control the entrance then offered surrender terms which Ludlow answered with a barrage of shot. Bowyer was mortally wounded but soon replaced by Colonel Barnes who threw up a fort on the hill that dominated the castle. Further attempts at negotiation failed, but by January the garrison's provisions were running low and the Royalists had made a number of breaches. In February more troops under Sir Francis Doddington with an engineer and some Mendip miners arrived to undermine the walls and lay charges. On 14 March one mine was prematurely exploded

*Mendip miner*

by the vibration of the castle guns, bringing down a large section of the tower wall including part of Ludlow's own chamber in which he was working. Drawing his sword he stood ready to defend the breach, but the enemy were equally surprised and failed to attack.

The garrison's condition was now hopeless, as the explosion had destroyed their stores, so again negotiations on surrender took place. Ludlow obtained reasonable terms, and on 18 March, he and his remaining 75 men surrendered.

*Musketeer*

# The Battle of Cheriton

## 29 March 1644

### *An unexpected and great victory*

**Waller camped in Lamborough fields, with his HQ at Hinton Ampner House.**

*Sir William Balfour*

Spring 1644 allowed the re-commencement of campaigning. Waller and Hopton both received reinforcements but in both cases led by officers who were senior in rank to them. The reinforcements from the Oxford army were brought by the King's senior general, Patrick Ruthven, Earl of Forth, a soldier of great experience, but aged and gout ridden.

Waller had been sent a new brigade of the London Trained Bands, and a force of cavalry and mounted infantry from Essex's army under Lieutenant General Sir William Balfour. Like Essex, Balfour did not get on with Waller, but they did cooperate in the forthcoming campaign.

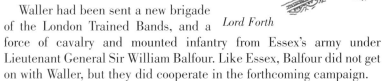

*Lord Forth*

His forces complete, Waller advanced towards Winchester where Hopton's army lay, but he was constrained by orders that he was 'not to engage except upon advantage'. The Royalists, alerted, drew up their forces east of Winchester, from whence scouts were sent to locate Waller. Contact was made at West Meon and then south of Cheriton village. Hopton guessing that Waller was heading towards Alresford to quarter, sent his own troops there first.

Finding Alresford occupied, Waller camped in Lamborough fields, south of Cheriton, with his HQ at Hinton Ampner House. Hopton now brought up his main body to Tichborne Down where they camped for the night.

*View of Cheriton Down from Hinton Ampner House*

Next morning both armies maintained their position but there was skirmishing between opposing patrols, and by night-fall a Royalist detachment of 1,500 men under George Lisle had set up an outpost on Cheriton Down overlooking Waller's camp. During the night there was so much noise from moving wagons that the Royalists began to believe Waller was withdrawing. The Royalist Council of War decided that whatever Waller was doing, they would attack next morning.

29 March dawned, and out of the mist came a surprise attack on Hopton's left flank from 1,000 musketeers and 300 horse. The Parliamentary troops seized Cheriton Wood, dominating Lisle's position, and forcing him to withdraw to the main army which was advancing two bodies; the left commanded by Hopton and the right by Forth (summoned from a game of cards in Alresford). Hopton's wing eventually drove the Parliamentarians off the ridge and the King's two generals decided not to advance off their strong position. Meanwhile Waller, like the Royalists, formed his infantry into two divisions with left and right flanks covered by cavalry.

Disaster struck the Royalists when a young officer in Forth's division, possibly Colonel Henry Bard, 'with more youthful courage than soldier-like discretion' led his infantry regiment to attack down the hill. They were caught in the open and destroyed by Haselrig's heavy cavalry. More of Forth's troops followed and were smashed. Meanwhile Hopton's flank was attacked by Sir William Balfour's cavalry supported by infantry.

With increasing pressure on the Royalist line, Forth and Hopton began an organised retreat through Alresford where their rearguard set part of the town on fire, allowing them to withdraw to Basing House before escaping. Waller's victory, although not recognised at the time, was one of the main turning points of the war.

**The Parliamentary troops seized Cheriton Wood.**

**Disaster struck the Royalists when a young officer led his infantry regiment to attack down the hill.**

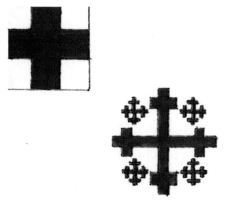

*Colonel Bard's Colour*

# The Siege of Lyme Regis

## *Mere breakfast work*

**The King had the 6,000 men of his nephew Prince Maurice, to attempt the port of Lyme Regis.**

*Prince Maurice*

The King had one army left in the West Country, the 6,000 men of his nephew Prince Maurice, who now moved to attempt the port of Lyme Regis which his officers thought could be taken in a morning.

Colonel Ceeley, governor of Lyme, commanded Colonel Were and Lieutenant Colonel Robert Blake, with 600 soldiers plus three or four hundred armed citizens. Only an earth bank and four turf forts protected their town which was completely dominated by hills on the landward side. On 20 April, Maurice demanded that the town should be given up to him. The Governor retorted that the German prince 'would do well to go back and settle in his own country'. He then sent out Blake with 200 defenders in an attack before the besiegers had set up camp, damaging guns and taking prisoners.

Two days of heavy assaults were made on the defences and Maurice raised a battery which threatened the western side of the town and its ancient breakwater, The Cobb. The defenders held their 'mud wall' and, 'the women of the town would come into the thickest of the danger to bring powder, bullet and provisions to the men'. On 26 April, two supply ships berthed in the harbour.

Maurice realised that he would be unable to starve the garrison so attempts were made to storm, but his infantry, 'being [local] forced men' were reluctant to fight. 'The horse was

*Lyme Regis housewife*

*The Cobb, Lyme Regis*

constrained to beat on the foot slashing and hewing them when they were put on any hard service else they have run away unto their homes'. Two more ships arrived during these attacks and landed a number of heavy guns and the welcome reinforcement of 100 men.

On 7 May, Maurice negotiated the removal and burial of his slain soldiers that lay in front of the defences. Permission was granted on condition that their arms and equipment were left to the defenders. On 22 May, Maurice launched a punishing attack upon The Cobb, burning over 20 vessels moored in its shelter before being repulsed.

The Earl of Warwick arrived the next morning on board his flagship James, with seven other Parliamentary warships. This put new heart into the defenders, especially as 300 sailors were put ashore to bolster the garrison. On 27 May, the Royalists came in great numbers, this time breaching the wall, allowing 1,000 men into the west of the town. They were only driven out again by the combined effort of the garrison, the newly arrived sailors, and the townswomen bearing muskets. This was the last major assault on the town, and on the night of 14/15 June, Maurice lifted the siege thanks to the resolve of the defenders and the news of the arrival of the Earl of Essex's army in Blandford. Essex had disobeyed Parliament's orders and had marched with the intention of relieving Parliamentary garrisons and crushing Royalist control of the south-west. Although initially successful, his mission was later to end in disaster at Lostwithiel in Cornwall.

*English warship of the 1640s*

*St Michael's Church, Lyme*

# The Siege of Basing House

## 1644

## *A house called Loyalty*

**Parliamentary forces began a formal siege.**

*John 5th, Marquiss of Winchester*

At the outbreak of the Civil War, Basing House was owned by John Paulet, the Catholic Marquiss of Winchester who decided, because of the house's strategic situation on the London/Exeter road, to refortify and garrison it for the King. His defences had withstood two assaults in 1643, but in spring of 1644, the House almost fell when the Marquiss's brother Edward was found to be in secret negotiations to deliver up Basing to Waller. It was expected that Lord Edward would be executed, but his sentence was commuted on condition that he hanged his fellow conspirators, which he did.

After sheltering Hopton's defeated forces from Cheriton, the Marquiss again prepared his house for defence and used his small force of cavalry to raid along the London Road. At the end of May, hearing that Parliamentary soldiers were preparing to billet in nearby Odiham, the Marquiss planned a night raid on the town, intending to burn it down. The attack was a disaster, for in the early hours of 1 June the advance guard of Royalists were spotted by Parliamentary scouts. In the confused skirmish that followed, the Marquiss lost nearly half of his force.

By 17 June, Parliamentary forces under Colonel Richard Norton began a formal siege. Norton's troops built four strong points; in St Mary's church to the east, one amongst old quarry workings on Cowdery's Down across the Loddon to the north, the third next to marshes in the west and to the south, a fort next to the present A30 road.

*Basing House outer walls showing musket loops*

The siege ran through the summer months with dwindling supplies, and an outbreak of smallpox compounding the sufferings of the garrison. Eventually the Marquiss's position had become so desperate that a woman messenger was sent to Oxford with pleas for help. The King was not yet returned from dealing with Essex in Cornwall, but his Oxford Council allowed a force to be raised to relieve Basing. The relief column of 600 men was commanded by the skilled Colonel Henry Gage, who got his force to a mile north of Basing before meeting the enemy. Gage hoped in vain for troops to join him from Winchester, so he was fortunate that 11 September dawned very misty and disguised his small numbers when he engaged Norton's forces. After two hours fighting on Cowdery's Down, Gage broke through to Basing House and for the next two days brought in food and ammunition before successfully withdrawing to Oxford.

Basing was soon under siege again from Norton and on 17 October the defenders witnessed the arrival of the armies of the Earls of Manchester and Essex.

Fortunately for the Marquiss, they were not there to join with the siege, but marching to try to trap the King at Newbury. The resulting 2nd Battle of Newbury was inconclusive and caused a rift in the Parliamentary high command, the result of which was a formation of a new army, the 'New Model'. At Basing, Norton gave up his siege due to bad weather.

**Colonel Henry Gage, who got his force to Cowdery's Down.**

*Colonel Henry Gage*

*Musketeer of Hawkin's Regiment, part of Gage's relief force*

A. THE OLDE HOVSE . B. THE NEW. C. THE TOWER THAT IS HALFE BATTERED DOWNE . D. THE KINGES BREAST WORKS . E. THE PARLIAMENTS BREAST WORKS.

*Contemporary view of the Siege of Basing House, 1644*

# The Siege of Taunton and Battle of Langport

## *The God of Heaven showed himself for Taunton*

**The Royalists withdrew temporarily to Bridgwater.**

*Colonel Robert Blake*

Taunton had no town walls, and was surrounded by flat fields with a network of hedges and lanes making it a difficult place for newly promoted Colonel Robert Blake to defend. Blake made his defence as close as possible, barricading streets and fortifying some houses. In the centre he created an inner line including the castle and St Mary Magdalene church.

On 27 September, the King, returning victorious from Cornwall, detached 3,000 men to help Sir Edmund Wyndham, governor of Bridgwater, 'to restrain Taunton'. Wyndham tried to storm it, but managed only to take the outer defences. The Royalists now attempted to starve the garrison out. The blockade lasted till 15 December when Wyndham was forced to lift the siege by the arrival of a Parliamentary relief force bringing food and ammunition before retiring.

By April 1645, Taunton was again besieged. Its relief a priority, Parliament sent their new Lord General, Sir Thomas Fairfax. Unfortunately Fairfax was recalled to the midlands but sent five thousand of his 'New Model' soldiers under Colonel Weldon onto Taunton where the defenders had been forced back to their second line again. Hearing of Weldon's rapid approach and thinking it to be Fairfax's entire army the Royalists withdrew. On 14 May, Weldon's brigade arrived and had their first day of rest; the men 'had scarce shoes with

*Part of Taunton Castle and reconstructed house of type destroyed in the siege*

any soales for them to tread upon'. But on 19 May the siege closed again, with Goring pitting over 9,000 men against the town. The Royalist conduct of this third siege was lax, allowing the defenders to bring in provisions, and after 14 June when news came in of the King's defeat at Naseby, many of Goring's infantry began to desert from what now was the largest force the King had left in the field. Goring withdrew from Taunton on 4 July to a more defendable position at Langport with the idea of eventually falling back to Bridgwater.

**Some of the defeated Royalists were set upon by country people who were part of a movement called the Clubmen, a developing third force in the war.**

The next day at Crewkerne, Blake and Weldon held a Council of War with Fairfax who had now returned, and it was decided that Weldon's brigade would join with Fairfax and pursue Goring. Blake returned to Taunton, his defence of which Lord Clarendon wrote, 'disappointed all our hopes, both in men and money in the great county, for it kept 4,000 foot and 5,000 horse employed nearly all the summer of 1645'.

It was the majority of this army that on 10 July prepared to face Fairfax's soldiers across Wagg Rhyne, east of Langport. Fairfax sent a cavalry charge led by Major Bethel crashing through a ford and up the hill towards Goring's main body. Bethel was forced back, but joined by more cavalry he renewed the attack with a fresh charge, breaking Goring's army, and forcing them to flee towards Bridgwater.

*Lord General Sir Thomas Fairfax*

Left: *New Model Army Sergeant*

*Langport battlefield from Goring's position*

# Clubmen

*More deeply tasted the misery of this unnatural and intestine war*

The Clubmen, named for their primitive weapons, arose in spring 1645 from the agricultural community; those who had 'more deeply tasted the misery of this unnatural and intestine war'. By May a meeting of over 4,000 agricultural workers and yeoman from Wiltshire and Dorset was held to set up an organisation of local watchmen to apprehend any wrong-doing soldiers, and Somerset farmers soon followed suit. As the movement became more militant it was claimed that by the use of church bells, nearly 20,000 men armed with 'muskets, fowling pieces, pikes, halberds, great clubs and suchlike' could be summoned. They would wear white ribbons in their hats to show their neutrality and peaceful desires, they having 'no other end but to defend themselves and their goods against all plunderers, and not to oppose either army'.

When Fairfax entered Dorset he confirmed his intention of keeping his army in good discipline by having one of his soldiers executed for plundering, and when he reached Dorchester he received a deputation from the Dorset Clubmen. Writing to Parliament, Fairfax described them as 'very confident of their cause and party', adding that the movement 'might be of evil consequence'.

**After Langport, Fairfax marched upon Bridgwater, but was confronted by 2,000 Somerset Clubmen.**

After Langport, Fairfax marched upon Bridgwater, but was confronted by 2,000 Somerset Clubmen, standing in good order and flying white colours made of sheets and aprons. Again Fairfax convinced them of his good intentions as well as persuading them to send provisions to the army for proper payment. The Clubmen saluted Fairfax with a ragged volley which one New Model soldier stated made 'many more afraid than of the shot in the battle the day before'.

Fairfax stormed Bridgewater on 23 July and his next objective was Sherborne, which Cromwell called 'a malicious, mischievous castle like its owner'. He arrived on 2 August and realised it would take weeks of a formal siege to reduce it. This was made increasingly difficult by the actions of the Dorset Clubmen whom Fairfax believed were acting on behalf of the Royalists. Fairfax's second-in-command

Right: *St Mary's Church, Shroton*
Far right: *Reconstruction of the Clubmen's Colours captured at Hambledon Hill*

IF YOU OFFER TO PLUNDER OR TAKE OUR CATTLE, BE ASSURED WE WILL BID YOU BATTLE

Lieutenant General Oliver Cromwell was given the task of stopping them, and set out on 4 August with 1,000 horse and dragoons to disrupt a suspect Clubman gathering at Shaftesbury. On his way he discovered over 2,000 militant Clubmen digging in on top of the Iron Age fort on Hambledon Hill. Seeking to avoid violence, Cromwell tried to negotiate but his messengers were fired upon and so he reluctantly gave the order to attack. The defenders fled, many were only kept in the ranks by the threats of their leaders, 'especially two vile ministers' who threatened to pistol any that lay down their arms. Unfortunately 60 men were killed but 400 Clubmen were taken prisoner and kept overnight in Shroton Church. Next morning, after a lecture from Cromwell, most were released, Cromwell describing them to Fairfax as 'poor silly creatures', and their movement dissolved.

*Lieutenant General Oliver Cromwell*

Sherborne Castle surrendered to Fairfax after six weeks, his soldiers looting it and selling their booty in Sherborne market the next morning.

*Hambledon Hill Iron Age hillfort*

*Sherborne Old Castle. 6,000 faggots of wood were needed by the attackers to fill and cross the ditch*

# Like Vipers in the Bowels

*Bristol, the most important Royalist garrison in the West*

**First was Devizes, next Lacock Abbey and Winchester.**

**Basing House was now the only Royalist stronghold in Hampshire.**

Once Sherborne fell, Fairfax closed upon Bristol, the most important Royalist garrison in the West. As governor of the city, Prince Rupert had assured the King that he could hold Bristol for at least 4 months. But on 10 September Fairfax's brigades attacked on all sides and Rupert surrendered.

With Bristol taken Fairfax began his preparation for an advance into Devon and Cornwall, but there were still Royalist fortresses in his rear which 'like vipers in the bowels infest the midland parts'. These were left to Cromwell to expunge with a force of 5,000 men and a train of heavy guns. Cromwell's first target was Devizes which surrendered on 23 September. Next came Lacock Abbey which agreed to surrender as long as it was to Fairfax in person. Cromwell now marched into Hampshire to face Winchester which surrendered to him upon arrival. The governor, Colonel Ogle, held on to the castle that dominated the town but it took just a few days for Cromwell's guns to break the walls. Ogle surrendered and he and his garrison were allowed to return to their homes.

Basing House was now the only Royalist stronghold in Hampshire

*Winchester West Gate*

*Marquiss of Winchester's Cornet*

*Siege gun on the move*

26

and had been besieged since August by Colonel John Dalbier, 'the cunning engineer'. Dalbier did not have enough men to storm Basing but he had done enough to make life a misery, including a poison gas attack. Cromwell joined him on 8 October and emplaced his guns including a 'cannon royal' which fired a 64lb ball. On 12 October Cromwell summoned Basing to surrender which the Marquiss refused.

Basing was stormed on the morning of 14 October, taking three quarters of an hour to complete the capture of the house which was consumed in flames. Cromwell wrote to Parliament, 'I thank God I can give you a good account of Basing'.

With Hampshire cleared, Cromwell rejoined Fairfax, on the way taking Langford Castle, Wiltshire's last Royalist outpost.

By 1646, few Royalists remained in Somerset and Dorset. Corfe Castle, dominating the pass through the Purbeck Hills was held by the widowed Lady Bankes. With a small garrison she had withstood a 13-week siege in 1643 and since October, she had held against Parliamentarian Colonel Bingham. In February 1646 a small cavalry force broke through to rescue her, but she refused to leave her home. The garrison was finally betrayed by one of its own officers, and on 26 February the castle was handed over to Bingham who permitted the defenders to return to their homes. Lady Bankes was allowed to keep the key to the castle as a symbol of her brave defence.

April saw the whole of Wessex in Parliament's hands and on 5 May King Charles surrendered. Parliament prepared to make a negotiated settlement for his return to the throne. It now looked as if the long years of war were over, but Parliament had forgotten about the people who had won that war for them, the officers and men of the New Model Army.

**Cromwell wrote to Parliament, 'I thank God I can give you a good account of Basing'.**

**April saw the whole of Wessex in Parliament's hands.**

*Lady Bankes, defender of Corfe Castle*

*Corfe Castle*

# A Royal Prisoner

*You have done your work boys, and may now go play, unless you fall out among yourselves*

*Colonel Robert Hammond*

On 21 March 1646, Sir Jacob Astley surrendered the last Royalist army, telling his captors, 'You have done your work boys, and may now go play, unless you fall out among yourselves'. And fall out is what they did; the Army with Parliament and the Parliament amongst itself. The Army took possession of Charles, taking him with them as they marched on London to demand their hard-won rights. When the New Model reached the capital on 6 August, negotiations were held and the King was lodged at Hampton Court Palace. Debates were held at Putney through the autumn, and radical decisions were made about the future, more democratic governance of the country, but on 11 November, the King made a mysteriously easy escape, and the results of the debate put aside.

Charles eluded capture, but failing to find a ship, found refuge at Titchfield Abbey. The King was in a quandary – could he find another ship to take him safely to the continent, or should he stay on English soil and exploit the cracks appearing in the ranks of his enemy? Charles decided on the latter and surrendered himself to the governor of the Isle of Wight, Colonel Robert Hammond. Hammond was an honourable man, and took the King to the Island, lodging him in the Constable's House at Carisbrooke Castle. He warned the King however,

*Titchfield Abbey*

*Carisbrooke Castle, Govenor's lodgings*

28

he would have to obey any orders issued to him from Parliament regarding Charles.

Now that the King was back in custody, the various factions once more began negotiations with him. At this stage, most parties desired the King back on the throne but with reduced powers.

Charles was allowed freedom to travel round the Island to visit friends, and a bowling green was built for him within the castle. But Charles deviously signed a secret agreement with visiting Scots commissioners for the 'raising of an Army for his Delivery and Restitution' whilst prolonging negotiations with Parliament and the Army, and sowing the seeds of a second civil war.

*Charles I*

The King himself made two unsuccessful attempts to escape and on 23 March large scale Royalist uprisings broke out in England and Wales, and on 8 July the Scots invaded. Fairfax dealt with the English Royalists whilst Cromwell destroyed the Scots at Preston.

Despite Charles's duplicity in these events, Parliament still wanted to negotiate with him, but the Army had had enough. On 30 November, the Army moved Charles to Hurst Castle, 'the worst castle in England' as he described it, and then three weeks later to Windsor. The Army purged Parliament of MPs who did not want to support it, and on 20 December brought Charles to trial in Westminster Great Hall, charged as a tyrant and traitor to his own people. Found guilty, Charles was executed at Whitehall on 30 January 1649.

A week later the monarchy was abolished and England became a republic. The Scots thought differently, for on 5 February, they proclaimed the Prince of Wales as King Charles II.

*Hurst Castle*

*In 1653 Oliver Cromwell became the Lord Protector of England*

**Cromwell, the new Lord General, utterly defeated Charles II at Worcester on 3 September 1651, the final great battle of the Civil War.**

In spring 1651 Charles II, with a mostly Scottish army, crossed the border hoping English Royalists would join him. He was however disappointed. Cromwell, the new Lord General, utterly defeated him at Worcester on 3 September 1651, the final great battle of the Civil War.

Charles escaped, but was now a hunted fugitive, sheltered by a number of Catholic families in the midlands. Plans were made to get him to Bristol and onto a ship to get him out of the country. Disguised as servant 'William Jackson', Charles rode before Jane Lane, daughter of a loyal household, to Abbot's Leigh near Bristol. During the next three days efforts failed to find a suitable ship, and Charles was almost recognised. Lord Wilmot joined the party, and suggested they travel to Francis Wyndham's house at Trent on the Somerset Dorset border and try to obtain a ship from a south coast port. Charles agreed and they reached Trent on 17 September. This remained their base for 18 days, during which time Jane returned home, and various schemes were tried to get him on to a ship. One plan was for Charles, with a small group, to pretend to be a runaway marriage party going to Charmouth to await collection to board a vessel at Lyme. Charmouth and Bridport were full of soldiers and Charles was recognised, so they fled to an inn in Broad Windsor for the night, only to find 40 soldiers there. Fortunately the soldiers were too busy with a woman who was giving birth, to pay attention to him and in the morning he returned unnoticed to Trent, having given up on this attempt.

*Charles II*

*Jane Lane and Charles II*

*Site of the inn at Broad Windsor*

The Dorset coast now seemed closed to Charles, so the Hampshire and Sussex ports were tried. The King moved to Heale House near Salisbury, remaining there for 7 days, one of which he spent hiding amongst the sarsens of Stonehenge when it was thought he had been spotted. At last a ship, the coal-brig *Surprise*, was found at Shoreham and Charles and Wilmot set sail on 15 October, disembarking the next day in Normandy.

In 1653 Oliver Cromwell became the Lord Protector of England and experimented with a number of forms of government, none of which pleased the Royalist or radical factions within the country and there were plots to overthrow him. The most serious one occurred in early 1655 when Colonel John Penruddock tried to raise Wiltshire in rebellion, but it was poorly supported, quickly suppressed, and the leaders executed.

*Colonel John Penruddock*

Cromwell ruled the country until his death in 1658. He was succeeded by his son Richard, who although an intelligent and honest man, could not hold the country together and was soon forced to stand down. In the subsequent chaos, the exiled Charles was invited to take the throne of a kingdom that was greatly changed, for England was now on the road to democracy, but by this stage the people were simply happy that 'this war without an enemy' had at last ended.

*Heale House*

# Acknowledgements

First published in the United Kingdom in 2015 by Wessex Books
Text © Alan Turton 2015
Design and layout © Wessex Books 2015
Cover artwork by KFD Ltd
Photographs by Nicola Turton
Line drawings by Alan Turton
Editorial assistance from David Allen, Curator of Hampshire Archaeology, Helen Burgess and Nicola Turton

Edited by Jane Drake
Wessex Books, 10 Thistlebarrow Road, Salisbury Wilts SP1 3RU
Tel: 01722 349695
Email: info@wessexbooks.co.uk
www.wessexbooks,co,uk
Front Cover Panel © Hampshire Cultural Trust

Printed in India

ISBN 978-1-903035-46-7

# Bibliography

Adair, John, Professor (ed), *They Saw it Happen: Contemporary Accounts of the Siege of Basing House*, Hampshire County Council, 1981

Barrett, John, *The Civil War in the South West*, Pen and Sword, Barnsley, 2005

Godwin, G.N., *The Civil War in Hampshire*, Laurence Oxley, Alresford, 1973

Jones, Jack D., *The Royal Prisoner*, Lutterworth Press, London, 1965

MacLachlan, Tony, *The Civil War in Wiltshire*, Rowanvale Books, Salisbury, 1997

Peachey, S., Turton, A., *War in the West (Part 1)*, Stuart Press, Bristol, 1994

Scott, Christopher L., *The Battles of Newbury*, Pen and Sword, Barnsley, 2008

Underdown, David, *Revel, Riot and Rebellion*, Oxford University Press, Oxford, 1985

Underdown, David, *Somerset in the Civil War and Interregnum*, David & Charles, Newton Abbott, 1973

Webb, John, *The Siege of Portsmouth in the Civil War*, The Portsmouth Papers, No. 7, Portsmouth, 1969

Wroughton, John, *The Battle of Lansdown 1643*, The Lansdown Press, Bath, 2008

Wroughton, John, *A Community at War*, The Lansdown Press, Bath, 1992